Mrs. Greenough

**Treason at Home**

A Novel: Vol. I.

Mrs. Greenough

**Treason at Home**
*A Novel: Vol. I.*

ISBN/EAN: 9783337065454

Printed in Europe, USA, Canada, Australia, Japan

Cover: Foto ©Andreas Hilbeck / pixelio.de

More available books at **www.hansebooks.com**

# TREASON AT HOME.

## A NOVEL.

### IN THREE VOLUMES.

BY

## MRS. GREENOUGH.

VOL. I.

London:

T. CAUTLEY NEWBY, PUBLISHER,

30, WELBECK STREET, CAVENDISH SQUARE,

1865.

# TREASON AT HOME.

## CHAPTER I.

TWILIGHT was settling over the landscape, as a young man, tall and athletic, turned into the deeper shadow of the avenue which led to Arden Hall. A carriage which servants were busily engaged in unpacking, stood before the open door. Quickening his pace he crossed the dark hall, and pausing for an instant on the threshold of the drawing-room, cast a quick glance on the persons within.

In a low easy chair sat his aunt, Mrs. Arden. She was a small, spare woman, with insignificant

features, and hair and complexion of a faded
straw colour; but this physiognomy, which
seemed intended by nature for the quietest of
*rôles*, was accompanied by two startled-looking
greenish-grey eyes, which had a habit of in-
cessantly roving hither, thither, and everywhere.
These eyes were placed beneath two scanty eyebrows, which, raised and permanently retained a
full half inch above their natural level, communicated an expression of distrustful expectation to
the rest of her face, an expression which in no
wise belied the habitual state of her mind. For
Mrs. Arden possessed an unbounded love of the
marvellous, and was endowed with an insatiable
appetite for all things melancholy and grievous
in the recital. Nor was this propensity dwarfed
by any want of proper sustenance. She breakfasted
with the "Times" in her hand, and devoured
muffins and manslaughters alternately. She
lunched upon the last sensation novel, and supped,
faithful to her ascending scale, on the ghostly
literature of the present and the past. Nothing

had proved too dry for her perseverance, did but the supernatural mingle largely enough with it. Works on necromancy, on astrology, on alchemy, crowded the shelves of her private bookcase, side by side with haunted legends of every country and every age. Nor was there any danger of this stream running dry. A new influx of the preternatural had recently made its way to Arden Hall. The lower cupboard of that same bookcase was crammed to overflowing with contemporaneous publications, principally from France, attesting positive and incontrovertible facts, so utterly astounding as, in Mrs. Arden's opinion, to throw all previous human experiences into the shade, proving spirits to be but men minus members, and triumphantly refuting the vulgar belief that Heaven is a place of rest.

Mrs. Arden, at this present time, though constantly on the *qui vive* for apparitions and visitations, had nevertheless been left to maintain her faith solely on the experiences of others. A good soul she was, *au reste*, kindly hearted, affectionate, and charitable ; her foibles in no wise diminishing the activity of her naturally amiable qualities, though occasionally prompting somewhat peculiar and obtrusive manifestations of the same.

But at the moment of her nephew's appearance on the threshold of the drawing-room, activity did not seem to be at all Mrs. Arden's mood. Her head inclined slightly on one side, she was contemplating with an expression of compassionate melancholy a young girl who sat leaning back upon the sofa, beside a man a little past the prime of life. Her scrutiny appeared to annoy her visitor, if one might judge by her resolutely down-cast eyes and constrained attitude.    The young man was not at that moment able to pursue his investigation further, for as, after his momentary pause, he advanced, the gentleman beside her rose and held out his hand.

A bald-headed, stately man was John Arden, with ample forehead, aquiline nose, and compressed lips. As his cold eye rested upon the young man, it took a colder gleam; as he smiled an answer to his greeting, a concealed sneer vibrated around his mouth. He was weighing him by his own standard, and noting how much he was wanting.

" Edith, my dear, your cousin Walter," said Mrs. Arden, as her nephew turned towards the girl.

She rose, curtseyed frigidly, without raising her eyes, then resumed her seat.

" What a strange old picture she looks like," thought Walter to himself, while in his frank, ringing voice he welcomed the new comer. Nor was the comment inappropriate.

The girl's small, pale features were framed in a mass of half-curled golden hair, the long lashes that rested on her colourless cheeks but partly concealed the dark circles beneath her eyes. The delicacy of her appearance was heightened by the richness of her attire. Her dress was trimmed with a profusion of ornament, manifestly unsuitable to her age.    She looked like some old portrait of a childish Infanta, which had lost its way, from some ancient palace, into life.

But a few words had been exchanged between the two men, when a strange maid presented herself at the door.

" Your room's ready, Miss."

" Bad face, that," thought Walter.

A very bad face it was.

Edith rose, and, raising her eyes for the first time looked wistfully in her father's face,—they were large, crystalline eyes, dark, but by the lamplight one could not see of what colour.

The hard visage of the banker softened as he looked at her.

" I must bid you good night and good-bye at once, my pet," he said, " for I start early, to take the train, you know."

" Come to my door to-morrow morning," she said, in a low voice, but not so low that it escaped the maid's ear.    " If you please, sir," she said, coming forward, " the doctor was very particular that Miss Arden was not to be disturbed in the morning."

Edith's **brows** contracted, her cheeks flushed a little.

" **You** won't disturb me, papa, I shall be awake."

**Her** father hesitated.

" Indeed, Miss—" the maid began.

Edith turned abruptly from her.

" Brenton knows best; I'm afraid," said Mr. Arden.

" Pray come," Edith repeated.

Her father yielded to the urgency of her tone. As he kissed her, she trembled visibly, but immediately recovering herself, with a reverence to Mrs. Arden, withdrew.

Silence followed her departure.

Her father seemed absorbed in painful thought. Walter sat recalling her singular appearance and wondering what sort of inmate she would prove,— the prospect was not promising, he was compelled

to confess,—while Mrs. Arden's face worked in
the way that betokened with her the advent of
some new idea.   She began to shift herself about
in her easy chair, to cross first the left toe of
her satin slipper over the right, and then the
right over the left, in rapid alternation ; her eyes
made the tour of the room several times, at each
return resting an instant on John Arden's face, as
if to ascertain whether he were in a mood for receiving what she had to say.   At length, as if they
could be withheld no longer, the words broke
from her.

" It's Lady Pettigrew's Panacea, that she
wants ! "

Mr. Arden looked up inquiringly, "I beg
your pardon.   What did you say ? "

" It's Lady Pettigrew's Panacea, that she
wants," repeated Mrs. Arden, with the air of a
Napoleon espying a weak point in the enemy's
centre.   " There never was anything like it.   It
works wonders.   There's nothing that it won't
do.   If you had only seen Walter when he first

came here ten years ago! He was almost as
tall as he is now, and so thin and so pale that it
was dreadful to look at him, positively dreadful.
I thought he wouldn't live, and I told his uncle
so; but, I said, there's one thing that may save
him, and that's Lady Pettigrew's Panacea, and I
mean to try it. His uncle thought it wouldn't
do him any good, but I wasn't going to see him
sink into his grave without a struggle, so I sent
off the next day and bought twelve bottles of it.
They lasted him about three months. I kept a
close look out, and as soon as one bottle was empty
I put another full one into his room, and so on
till they were all gone. He complained a little
the first day or two, but he soon got used to the
taste, and said no more about it, and by the time
the twelve bottles were finished he looked like
another creature. I never can be grateful enough
to Lady Pettigrew's Panacea, never!"

Walter made no comment on his aunt's
harangue, unless a certain twitching of his brown
moustache might be considered as such. He had

never judged it expedient to inform her that he
had, on the third day after his arrival at Arden
Hall gone privately to his uncle and informed
him that he would prefer returning to the Rev.
Paul Overteach and being worked to death, to
remaining at the Hall and being poisoned by Lady
Pettigrew's Panacea; and that Mr. William
Arden had sympathized with him, and had proposed, by way of avoiding anything which might
be painful to his aunt's feelings, to administer
the daily wine-glass full of the mixture to an
arbor vitæ tree which grew beneath his
window, the robustness of whose constitution
might be considered to guarantee it against the
pernicious influence of the application. For this
Walter had compounded, and in a few weeks the
improvement in his health justified the wisdom
of Mr. Arden's advice, while at the same time,
by a singular contradiction, it gave occasion to
Mrs. Arden to enforce on every opportunity, with
that certainty given by ocular demonstration, the
invigorating effects of Lady Pettigrew's Panacea.

"Lady Pettigrew's Panacea," repeated Mr. Arden. " No, I don't think she has tried that. She has taken Dr. Williams' tonic, and Bridge's bitters, and Dr. Lowood's bracing extract, and Sir Joseph Slingsby's strengthening mixture, but I don't think she has ever tried that."

" Then she had better begin it to-morrow," re-joined Mrs. Arden, her eyes shining with antici-pated triumph. " Oh, it will make quite a different creature of her, you will see. Why, there was Mrs. Wilcox's baby, as soon as I advised three drops of the panacea a day, it be-gan to rally, and it was the most miserable, starved-looking little object before that you ever saw. The Dean said it was because he insisted on having the wet nurse changed, but that was all nonsense; I knew better." And Mrs. Arden shook her head with an air of cutting contempt at the narrow-minded incredulity of the Dean.

The precipitation which his sister-in-law car-ried into her good intentions, appeared to dis-compose Mr. Arden, and he took advantage of the next pause in her record of miraculous cures, to state that the physicians had expressly ordered that his daughter should try no more remedies, but depend solely upon country air and quiet for her restoration.

Mrs. Arden made no reply. She was easily silenced, for she was, as we have said, a timid woman; but she sat revolving in her mind the bigotry of London physicians, the hard hearted folly of her brother-in-law, and the cruel fate of Edith, who in the very house with seven bottles of Lady Pettigrew's Panacea, was not to be permitted a single drop of that elixir.

The current of her reflections was interrupted by Mr. Arden, who was becoming apprehensive lest his declining to submit Edith to a course of domestic treatment had seriously offended his sister-in-law.

"The physicians assure me that with entire change of air and scene she will probably in time regain her health without the aid of medicine. Nothing short of the absolute necessity of the case would have induced me to make the call upon your kindness that I have done, and, believe me, I am deeply grateful."

Mr. Arden, though not prone to be embarrassed, spoke these words awkwardly; indeed there was sufficient cause for embarrassment. He had broken off all intercourse with his elder brother's widow from the time of that brother's death. William Arden having regained, by his own exertions, the family estate which, being unentailed, had slipped from the impoverished grasp of his father, had considered himself entitled to leave it to his wife, and after her death to her orphan nephew, his son by adoption. John Arden, the rich banker, though possessing a much finer place of his own, considered himself aggrieved thereby, and, as has been said, had testified his displeasure by dropping all intercourse with the Hall. But when Edith fell ill, and change of place and society seemed to be the one thing needful, John Arden bethought himself of the Hall, and of his sister-in-law, of whose talents as a sick

nurse he had had evidence, his wife having, many
years before, fallen ill when on a visit there, and
having been tended by Mrs. William Arden with
devoted care.    Accordingly, he had indited a
letter, requesting leave to send Edith to Arden
Hall for a visit, alleging the extreme delicacy of
her health as the reason for the request.    Mrs.
Arden had received that letter with as much
indignation as her yielding disposition would
allow, at the circumstance that the intercourse
so long dropped was now renewed from so
palpably selfish a motive.    But affectionate re-
membrance of Edith's mother, and compassion for
the young invalid whom she only remembered as
a shy, but rosy child, prevailed over her annoyance,
and she despatched a cordial invitation to her niece.

"I am deeply grateful," Mr. John Arden had
said.

"Oh, dear me, there's no occasion for you to be
grateful at all, not the least.    I do it for Maria's
sake.    She was a sweet woman, very," responded
Mrs. Arden, with that appalling frankness into

which easily fluttered persons are sometimes inadvertently impelled.

Reply to such a statement would have been difficult. Mr. John Arden did not attempt it. Perhaps he cared little on what ground Edith was received, so long as received she was. His next remark was addressed to Walter.

" Are there any young people in the neighbourhood whom she would be likely to know?"

" There are men enough," said Walter, slightly arching his eyebrows. " But there's a great dearth of girls in this part of the country. Lady Tremyss's daughter is the only one within three miles."

" Is she near Edith's age?"

" About the same, I fancy, though Miss Isabel looks much older."

" And Lady Tremyss, does she keep her good looks? I remember her as one of the handsomest women in London."

" As handsome as ever, though Miss Isabel's face is more to my taste."

"Strangely reserved Lady Tremyss was. I used to think it was owing to Sir Ralph's jealous temper."

"I should rather think it natural. It has grown on her since his death. That was a great shock to her. You remember the circumstances?

"Perfectly."

And Mr. John Arden, who shared the repugnance to any mention of death, which is characteristic of men of his stamp, exchanged the subject for the more welcome one of the improvements he had planned and was executing at Arden Court, and a list of the distinguished guests who were about to honour it with their presence,—a theme on which and on whose ramifications he complacently dilated till bed-time.

## CHAPTER II.

THE sun was shining brightly the next morning, as young Arden, returning from an early
walk, passed beneath the breakfast-room window.
A pleasant fellow he was, this Walter Arden,
with his tall figure, his broad shoulders, his open
eye, and his manly, well-cut features. He was,
moreover, the best rider, wrestler, and runner in
the county; and though, to his shame be it
spoken, but an indifferent billiard player, his
game of chess was so masterly as to vindicate
the assertion of his tutor when at Cambridge,
that if he had given half the time to mathematics
that he devoted to boat racing, he would have
been sure of taking a first.

Looking up as he advanced, he saw Edith, her gaze fixed absently upon the sunny sweep of the lawn. He stopped and called up a cordial good morning. She lowered her eyes to where he stood, bowed slightly, and turned away.

"You are up early," he said, gaily, as he entered the breakfast-room, "Your aunt is not yet down."

"Papa went at six," she answered, coldly, but with a regretful cadence in her voice.

"It's a fine day; he will have a pleasant trip."

"I hope so," she replied, in a more gracious tone.

"By the time he comes again we will have you quite a different person, as rosy as a milkmaid," said Walter, looking compassionately down upon his companion.

She scanned his face for a moment.

"I think I shall like to stay here," she said, slowly, as if making up her mind aloud.

"Of course you will. It's the jolliest place in

the world—at least, I think it so. We shall make you like it so much, that you will never wish to go away," replied her cousin, over-shooting the mark.

The chilly reserve, a moment dissipated, closed again over Edith's face. She shook her head, and silently returned to her post by the window.

" What's the matter with her, I wonder? I wish Aunt Arden would come down," thought Walter. " I feel as if somebody had given me a butterfly to hold. I have vexed her, that's plain enough, but I'll be shot if I know why."

As he stood, palpably annoyed, Edith turned, looked up, and smiled. The change was marvel-lous; the girl's face became flooded with beauty.

" You meant kindly," she said, " Don't mind when I'm cross."

At this moment Mrs. Arden rustled into the room. There were traces of vexation on her face, though she was doing her best to conceal them. Before long, however, the cause of disturbance came out.

"So I hear your maid has gone back, my dear," she said, as they took their places at the breakfast table.

"Yes," replied Edith, briefly.

Mrs. Arden coughed uneasily.

"I hope nothing had gone wrong to make her unwilling to remain at the Hall; I should be quite distressed if I thought so."

"She wanted to stay, I believe," responded Edith.

"Really; then might I ask?—I should be glad to know.—I hope there was nothing that you would have preferred differently arranged, my dear. I thought the room was very nice for her," said Mrs. Arden, who had been grievously discomposed by intelligence communicated by Nitson, her maid, whilst dressing her, to the effect that Miss Arden's maid had taken her departure from the Hall with Mr. John Arden, looking 'as cross as two sticks.'

"It wasn't that, at all. The room was much prettier than the one she has at home. It was

only because I did'nt want her. I told papa
that you would very likely know of some
one—a quiet little country girl is what I would
like."

Mrs. Arden turned her eyes upon the daintily
arranged curls and careful toilette of her niece,
with a look of dismay.

"Oh! but I'm afraid you haven't considered,
my dear! Indeed, I'm quite sure you haven't. I
couldn't find anyone here to do your hair that
way, and to make you look as you do now. I'm
afraid you'll find it a great disappointment. And
I don't know of any one, except little Letty
Prast, and she is a good, quiet, tidy little thing,
but she's had a hard life, what with her sick
mother and her drunken father; and now her
mother's dead, and her father's on the parish,
and it would be such a nice place for her. But
then, she wouldn't do for you at all, my dear,
not at all. She was never in service, except
once, as one of the under housemaids at the
Park," said Mrs. Arden, recollecting herself,

" she wouldn't know the names of half the things you wear."

"How old is she?" enquired Edith, apparently not to be deterred from prosecuting her enquiries by Mrs. Arden's account of Letty Prast's deficiencies.

" I think she must be twenty.  Yes, it's five years ago this spring that I gave her a gown to be confirmed in, and then she was fifteen.  She's just about twenty, now."

" You said, I think, that her mother was dead."

" Yes ; and she almost broke her heart about it, although she was nothing but a slave to her while she lived, for her mother wasn't a good tempered woman at all, and used to scold her from morning till night.  I used quite to pity the poor girl, I did indeed.  I can't bear to see anyone made unhappy."

Edith turned a penetrating glance upon her aunt's face.  Her tone was softer, as she resumed—

"Then you think she would be affectionate?"

"Yes," replied Mrs. Arden, looking more and more puzzled at the drift of her niece's enquiries, " but then, my dear, you have been used to something very different from all this in your maid."

"If you please, I should like you to engage her for me; I think she is what I want," Edith quietly replied.

And Mrs. Arden, once satisfied that her niece's mind was not to be changed, began to lay plans for an immediate high-pressure education of Letty Prast by Nitson, so that she might as rapidly as possible be fitted for her unexpected elevation, to all of which her niece listened placidly, but without any apparent interest.

Walter took advantage of the opportunity afforded him by Edith's attention being directed to his aunt, to study her appearance more closely than he had hitherto been able to do. She appeared about fifteen, though she was, in fact, two years older. She was of the average height, but

extremely slender.   Her eyebrows and lashes
were of a much  darker  tint  than  her  hair, increasing the apparent depth of  her  eyes.   There
was something very peculiar in those eyes.  When
seen fronting the light, you would have said they
were of the exact hue of harebells ; when seen in
shadow  you would have sworn them to be black.
The irid had a way of suddenly and brilliantly
expanding when any emotion touched her, so
that the whole eye seemed filled with light.   The
rest of the features were delicate and regular,
but one's look did not rest long on them, it was
irresistibly drawn back to those deep, shadowy
eyes, so full of thought and sentiment, so
strangely contradicting the cold and somewhat
haughty expression of the rest of her face.

She looked as if there might be a great deal in
her to study, if one could only get at it.   He
would try to make her talk.

He profited by a momentary cessation of his
aunt's fine patter of conversation, to make the
attempt.

It proved unsuccessful—Edith either would not or could not talk. Nothing but monosyllables were to be obtained from her, and Walter, completely baffled and somewhat disgusted, betook himself, as soon as breakfast was over, to the stables and a cigar.

For the next few days he paid Edith as small attention as politeness would allow, but little by little he found himself watching and studying her. There was certainly something very peculiar about her—she was a regular enigma. It was long before he could make her out at all. She was constantly surprising and perplexing him. She would endure being fidgeted and fussed over by her aunt with unchanging resignation, never betraying vexation by look or sign. She underwent with the patience of a martyr, all the annoyances inflicted upon her by the awkwardness of her new maid—annoyances so grievous that the sympathizing Nitson at length broke into vicarious revolt.

"I don't see, mem, how Miss Arden can

stand it as she does," declared Nitson to her
mistress, " that girl's fingers are all thumbs.
She puts on Miss Arden's stays crooked, and
skips half the lacings in her boots every day of
her life, and tangles and twitches her hair enough
to make a statue scream, mem ; and Miss Arden
sits there and never opens her lips. Yesterday,
I couldn't stand by and see it any longer, and I
just took her beautiful long hair into my own
hands, and curled it, and did it up for her, and
she gave a little sigh when I got through, as if
it felt so good not to have it pulled ; and really I
haven't the strength to bear it any longer, mem,
and if you and Miss Arden are pleased, I should
be thankful to dress her every day. It's a real
pleasure to be near such a sweet young lady as
she is, mem, and if you think well, mem, Letty
can go into the laundry, for they want another
maid there, and Mrs. Pomfret was going to
speak to you to-day about it, and so Letty won't
lose her place, for she's a well-meaning girl, and
cries herself to sleep every night because she's so

stupid, which isn't no ways her own fault you
know, mem, so I feel as if she ought to be pre-
tected."

A conversation which Mrs. Arden related with
amplifying comments to Walter, just at the
moment when he was smarting under a tart
reply of Edith's to some perfectly inoffensive
remark as he had thought. No, he could not
understand her. In singular opposition to her
usual long suffering mildness or precocious
philosophy, would occasionally come a burst of
petulance, a mood of depression, a fit of silence,
so uncalled-for and unaccountable, as to throw
Walter entirely out in his calculations, and to set
at naught all the theories he had been forming as
to her character.

Yet the explanation was simple enough. From
the time of her mother's death Edith had been
bullied by her maid and tyrannized over by her
governess, both, in their way, equally clever and
unprincipled women, who had managed to secure
Mr. Arden's confidence. Under their joint op-

pression, Edith's spirits and health had broken down. But, little by little, the quiet of the Hall, the affectionate care of her aunt, and the healthy moral atmosphere about her, toned both body and mind to a more natural key. She grew stronger week by week, so that before long her rides on the little white pony which Mrs Arden had bought for her, extended their limits from half-an-hour's pacing round the Close to excursions of two or three miles. Walter was her attendant on these excursions, Mrs. Arden being afraid to entrust her to the care of any servant.

From looking upon these walks beside his cousin's pony as a nuisance, Walter came by degrees to consider them pleasures. Edith's reserve wore insensibly away. One day she told him something of her past miseries, in listening to which, Walter used expressions more energetic than elegant. Edith was not shocked, as she ought to have been; on the contrary, from that time she began to treat him as a friend.

When she had been a little more than a month

at the Hall, Walter proposed to take her as far as the gates of Ilton Park, closed for the time by the absence of the family.

"I'm sure I don't know what to say," said Mrs. Arden, on the afternoon of the projected excursion, looking dubiously up at the threatening sky, and then, equally dubiously contemplating Edith. "I really don't know what to say," she repeated, turning her eyes, with a rapid, rotatory motion, upon the weathercock, the pony, Walter, and Edith.

"Then we're off," said Walter, turning to place Edith in the saddle.

"Not if Aunt Arden says No," Edith replied.

" Dear me, child, I can't say No about anything to you, you know I can't," responded Mrs. Arden, piteously. "But Walter, if any ill comes of it, I shall lay it all on your shoulders."

And having partially satisfied her mind by this shifting of responsibility, Mrs. Arden watched, well pleased, from the hall steps, the departure of the two.

Winding through pleasant lanes bordered by fragrant hedge-rows, they reached at length the road which led by Ilton Park. On one side rose the dark stone wall enclosing the heavy woodland, on the other a low hedge and a narrow strip of green alone separated the way from the river, which flowed in gleaming eddies between its sloping banks. A few steps brought them to the pine shadowed gates of the park. On either side of the iron gateway, upon a massy pedestal of red sandstone, a sphinx lay couched, looking with stony gaze upon the river. The lodge was concealed from sight; the eye passing between the sphinxes, met but the shadows of the long avenue within. Walter stopped the pony, while Edith's eyes settled, as if fascinated, upon the faces of the sphinxes.

"It was an odd idea to put a woman's head on such a body," said Walter. "Beauty, strength, and ferocity ; that's what the compound means, I suppose."

"They look as if they knew something," said

Edith, glancing by them. " I wish they would say what it is."

" I'm afraid you won't be gratified. Whatever they know, they seem disposed to keep to themselves; and on the whole I think they're right. Just fancy being obliged to tell all they've seen since the time of the Pharaohs ! "

" Please, I would rather go on," said Edith, after a short silence, turning from the gate, with its mute sentinels.

As they came to a corner of the road, which still skirted the park, Walter, who was walking with his eyes on the ground, was startled by a faint cry from Edith. He hastily looked up.

Before them was a gigantic, black coated negro, his face traversed by a ghastly scar. Respectfully touching his hat, he passed them, and disappeared through a small door in the park wall, which he opened with a private key.

" What, afraid of Goliath ! " said Walter, seeing the disturbance on Edith's face. " He's the best creature in the world."

" Who is he, and how did he come here ? "

" He's the butler at Ilton Park.  Old Lady
Tremyss, Sir Ralph's mother, to whom the park
belonged, had estates in Jamaica, and that's
the way Goliath came to be here.  She brought
him."

" But he is so tall, and that dreadful scar ! "

" I said he is the best creature in the world,
and that scar proves it.  Not long before Sir
Ralph's death he got into one of his rages with
Goliath, and threw a decanter in his face, and cut
him as you saw, and for all that, Goliath risked
his life to get him out of the river, the night he
fell in."

" And did he save him ? "

" No.  The river is deep, and dangerous.
Goliath was alone.  He did all he could, but he
couldn't manage it."

" How did Sir Ralph get in ? " pursued Edith,
with a glance at the silent river.

" He was riding home late from a dinner party,
and chose to swim the river instead of going

round by the bridge. He was always a dare-devil on horseback."

" Why did not the groom help ? "

" As ill luck would have it, the groom got dead drunk that night, and Sir Ralph came home alone."

" What a terrible thing," said Edith, " to die in the cold and darkness so close to one's home." She shivered.

" Yes, but don't think of that, think what a good fellow Goliath showed himself."

" Yes, it was noble of him—to forgive Sir Ralph would have been much, but to risk his life for him —" She paused.

"A white servant would'nt have done it, but that race is different. Their fidelity seems like that of dogs,—pat them or kick them, they love you all the same."

" I don't think Goliath looks like that," Edith slowly replied, " I think it must have been something deeper."—She stopped a moment, then added, penitently, " I hope he didn't see how startled I was.   I should be so sorry to hurt his feelings."

"Oh, never mind.   If he did see it, it's no matter.   Goliath is such a good fellow !"

" I wish I had thought to ask him when the family is coming back," Walter resumed, after they had gone on a few steps.   " If you don't mind I'll run back and ask at the lodge."

He returned in a moment, his face glowing. Edith looked attentively at him.

" They will be here on Saturday evening.   I am glad they're coming.   Isabel will be a capital companion for you."

" Thank you, I don't care for any companions," Edith coolly answered, and Walter obtained only curt replies during the rest of her ride.

# CHAPTER III.

" Do you think Lady Tremyss will be at church to-day ? " asked Edith, as the carriage drove up to the church door on the next Sunday.

" Of course, my dear. Lady Tremyss is very punctual in her attendance. She and Isabel are always at morning service, though, I'm sorry to say, when the sermon is long Isabel fidgets dreadfully."

The carriage door was thrown open as she spoke, and they entered the little church.

Edith had not until that day been considered strong enough to undergo the fatigue of sitting through the service, and it was with an observant eye that she noted all around her.

The walls of a yellowish brown tint, the time worn and blackened oaken wood work, the high square pews with their curtains of crimson moreen, the curiously carved pulpit with its alternating lion's and angel's heads, the subdued and reverential faces of the cottagers who filled the benches; all these she saw through the vague and misty light that fell through the window at the extremity of the aisle, whose small and dusty panes seemed to esteem it their sole duty to guard against the entrance of the sunlight. All was dim, sombre, and hushed.

Edith placed herself where her eye could command the entrance. Never before had she been so anxious to see anyone as now to see Isabel. She had been seated but a few moments, when a lady, richly dressed in black, accompanied by a young girl, appeared on the threshold, and passing up the aisle, entered a pew a little beyond Mrs. Arden's. Edith instinctively recognized Lady Tremyss. She looked but at her. She had forgotten Isabel.

Features of faultless regularity, over which was spread an even tint of pale olive relieved by touches of red on the lips, and at the corners of the long black eyes; straight black hair smoothly parted on the low, compact forehead; a figure of the medium height, though in its stateliness appearing somewhat taller,—such was the presence that glided past Edith, riveting her attention with a painful fascination.

Lady Tremyss took her place, and sat motionless during the rest of the service, save that she rose when others rose, and knelt when others knelt. Yet this immobility suggested no thought of lassitude or weariness; it was not the indifference of ennui nor the nonchalance of indolence; it seemed the stillness of concentration, the visible expression and bodying forth of will. Had an acute observer been asked to analyze Lady Tremyss' emotionless face, to read the expression of her stirless figure, the result of his study would have been given in one word,—Intensity.

But there are few acute observers; and had the

vast majority of her acquaintance been questioned as to Lady Tremyss, they would have considered that they had made an exhaustive statement, in answering that she was a remarkably beautiful, quiet sort of woman, with distinguished manners, and a fine fortune ; those who most frequently visited the Park, adding, *par parenthèse*, that she was extraordinarily fond of her daughter, her only child.

As the effect produced on Edith's imagination by Lady Tremyss' strange and striking beauty began to lose its novelty, she turned her eyes on the figure by her side. That must be Isabel. But Edith could only discover that she was graceful, and her dress elegant. She waited with impatience for the end of the service, but, as usually happens when the fulfilment of our desires depends upon the movements of others, when the moment came she was disappointed. As Lady Tremyss and her daughter turned to pass down the aisle, Mrs. Arden, addressed by an antiquated lady in the pew above, interposed her figure between Edith and the object of her attention, effectually concealing Isabel from sight. When the colloquy was ended, and Edith at last reached the porch, Lady Tremyss and her daughter had already driven away.

The experiment of taking Edith to church did not quite fulfil Mrs. Arden's expectations. Perhaps the change of seeing her in *toilette de ville* instead of her customary straw hat and cambric dress, imprinted more strongly than usual on her aunt's perceptions the fact of her charge's peculiar delicacy of appearance; perhaps the girl was really over fatigued. However that may have been, after removing with her own hands the transparent bonnet and gauzy mantle, insisting on her swallowing a dose of sal volatile and water, which nearly choked her, and forcing her to take her luncheon reclined on a chaise longue instead of sitting at the table, as she wished to do, Mrs. Arden conduted her to her room, and depositing her on the bed, after pouring Eau-de-

Cologne on her handkerchief and carefully closing the curtains, left her with fervent entreaties that she would take a good nap, and look well rested at dinner time; an injunction there was little doubt but that Edith would obey to the best of her ability, enforced as it was by a reference to the possible necessity of a further dose of sal volatile and water.

When Edith descended to the dinner table, she was met by the information that Lady Tremyss and Isabel had called, and that Isabel had seemed very sorry not to have seen her; which, although a truthful, was still not a literal statement, Isabel having impetuously inquired for Edith as soon as she entered the drawing room, and having testified exceeding disappointment when told that she was lying down.

"I think she is the sweetest creature I ever saw in my life. I never took my eyes off her as I came up the aisle. She looked just like a seraph, with her great eyes and golden hair streaming out, only that seraphs are not all done up in lace and muslin, I suppose. It is too bad that I can't see her."

"Isabel was quite charmed," said Lady Tremyss, in her calm, still voice.

"Pray how old is she?" interposed Isabel.

"How old is she? my dear, why she's seventeen."

"What, is she actually older than I am? I should never have thought it. And how long has she been here? and how long is she going to stay? and you mean to have me a great deal with her, don't you? there's a darling, and I will be so good! and I'll never paint the chickens again."

A reference to a former exploit of Isabel's, who had used up a cake of vermilion in depicting various ghastly wounds upon some promising Dorkings, Mrs. Arden's especial pets, thereby drawing upon herself more lasting indignation than Mrs. Arden had ever before been known to express.

" Dear me, I really—"

Isabel stopped the long answer which she saw impending, by enquiring for Walter.

" Oh no, don't send. I'll go and find him."

She darted through the window, and finding Walter, descanted upon Edith's loveliness until it was time to return.

" Now do bring her early, there's a dear, and let her stay all the afternoon, do," said Isabel, as Mrs. Arden consented to Lady Tremyss' request that Edith should come the next day to call at the Park.

" I am sorry, but I'm really afraid I can't," replied Mrs. Arden. " I must first go to see Mrs. Moultrie, and she isn't strong enough to drive so far. She is so delicate, you haven't any idea. It quite frightens me sometimes, and then you know I haven't her in my own hands. Ah, if I could only take the right sort of care of her !"

And Mrs. Arden sighed, remembering Lady Pettigrew's Panacea.

" Couldn't you leave her at the Park on the way?" suggested Walter, glancing at Isabel's disappointed face.

" We will be very careful of her," added Lady Tremyss.

" I'll put her on the top shelf of my wardrobe, and cover her over with satin paper, if you like," urged Isabel, " only do please let her come."

And Mrs. Arden, who hated to say no, consented.

\*      \*      \*      \*

" You don't feel shy at being left here all alone, do you, my dear ?" asked Mrs. Arden, as the carriage passed between the couchant sphinxes, and entered the long, dark avenue of pines. "I used to be dreadfully shy at your age, I remember."

" No, I never feel shy," replied Edith. " I am so used to company, you know."

" I never feel shy," Edith had answered. She would rather have been seared with hot irons

than have confessed to her aunt that the vision of
Goliath had haunted her dreams all night, and
that she was at that instant internally trembling
with the dread of seeing him again, good though
he was.

Isabel met them in the hall.   Hurriedly greeting Mrs. Arden, she seized Edith by the hand.

" I am so glad you are come !   I so wanted to
know you !"

Following Mrs. Arden, she led Edith into the
drawing-room.

It was a long, low, dark apartment, the pre-
vailing colours crimson and black.    The old
pictures on the dark, polished walls glowed
duskily from their frames of carved ebony ; the
antique bronzes in the corners looked down
from high pedestals of *rosso antico;* an air of
sombre luxury reigned throughout.

Lady Tremyss rose from her tapestry frame as
they entered, courteously welcoming her guests.
Edith knew that she had taken her hand and
spoken a few sentences, but, to save her life, she

could not an instant after have recalled a single word her hostess had said. Her whole attention had been absorbed by that strange, still face: those long, black eyes had held her as by a charm.

As Lady Tremyss turned again to Mrs. Arden, Isabel drew Edith to the other end of the room and seated herself by her side.

" I have been expecting you, I don't know how long. I wanted to see you again."

The two girls fixed their eyes reciprocally on each other's face.

No stronger contrast than they presented could have been imagined. Isabel, tall, brilliant, sparkling, glowing with life ; her brown eyes smiling as if in rivalry with her mouth, an air of petulant gaiety, of mischievous playfulness glancing over her face ; and Edith, her deep eyes gazing earnestly forth from her transparent countenance, her serious lips gently but firmly closed, her golden curls falling over her delicate figure.

Isabel's mirthful eyes took a shade of gravity as they dwelt on her companion.

" I hope you mean to like me," she said, half imploringly, as if becoming aware that Edith's liking was mainly dependent on her will to like.

"I think I shall," Edith replied tranquilly, returning her companion's gaze.   In that brief question and reply their mutual standing was tacitly agreed upon.

" Mamma," said Isabel, when Mrs. Arden had taken her leave, " Miss Arden says she likes flowers.   I am going to take her to see my garden."

She led Edith to the terrace which skirted the southern side of the house.

Edith paused to look at the architecture of the mansion.   It was a long, irregular structure, which had apparently remained intact since the time of its erection.   The projecting gables, the oriel windows, with their small, lozenge-shaped panes, the high stacks of chimneys ornamented

with grinning heads, all proclaimed the date
" 1520," as plainly as did the little black and
yellow tiles set into the grey stone wall over the
hall door. Tall pines of still greater antiquity
bordered the quiet terrace, stretching out their
many tiered branches as if pointing at the house.

As Edith's eye passed slowly down the façade,
it caught, through one of the drawing-room windows, Lady Tremyss' black-robed figure, bending
over her embroidery frame. Edith moved on.

A few steps brought her to a glass door of great
width, to which two or three steps gave access.
The upper panes were of stained glass, and
represented various heraldic devices. That in
the centre was larger than the rest. It bore a
mailed hand grasping a blood-red rose. A heavy
creeper hung its festoons around, its dark green
wreaths contrasting with the rich tints of the
pictured panes.

" How pretty that is," said Edith, stopping.

" What? Oh, that stained glass. Yes, I suppose it is pretty. I never look at it. They're

the different coats of arms that married the Tremyss coat of arms. Sir Ralph had them put there when he came here to live."

" Then he didn't always live here ? "

" Oh, no ; when he was a bachelor he lived chiefly at the family place, Tremyss Hough, but mamma liked this best, so after he was married the other place was shut up, and now it has gone to the heir, of course. But don't stop now. I want you to see my garden."

She drew Edith to the extremity of the terrace, which opened on a small, but exquisitely arranged flower garden.

" This is beautiful," said Edith. " I am glad you brought me. What lovely azaleas, what beautiful fuchsias, and what a fine orange tree ! "

" Yes, that's Madame Ripetti," replied Isabel. " I have the leaves washed every day to keep her nice and clean."

" Madame Ripetti ? " repeated Edith.

" She planted it for me, and made it grow, so I call it after her. She was my governess."

"Then you liked her?" questioned Edith, whose feelings towards Madame Lourmel had not been precisely of a nature to induce her to keep alive her memory in a flower-pot.

"Oh, anybody would have liked her. She was a round, rosy little woman, very fond of little cakes, and very much afraid of earwigs and spiders. And, do you know, it was the most astonishing thing, the quantity of earwigs and spiders that used to get into her room when she first came here! I told her they came to help her eat the cakes she used to smuggle up. She kept the housemaids running half the time. It used to be so funny to see her standing on a chair in the middle of the room screaming 'Santa Vergine!' while the maids were hunting in every corner with brushes and dustpans. But at last I fell ill. I tumbled off my pony into a brook one day, and caught a dreadful cold. I was so hoarse that I couldn't speak, and so choked that I couldn't breathe. Mamma never went to bed for a week, nor did Madame Ripetti either.

She helped mamma and Melvil all she could, and when there was nothing else for her to do, she sat behind the bed curtains crying. She thought I couldn't see her, but I heard her sniff. Well, wasn't it curious? when I got well, although I saw that she always had a plate piled full of little cakes in her room, the earwigs and spiders had lost all their appetite for them. None were ever found there again. Wasn't that peculiar?"

Isabel laughed.

"It was peculiar that she never found you out," answered Edith. "But how could you touch them? I couldn't touch anything ugly if I tried."

"Oh, I didn't mind, I had on gloves you know. Besides, I like to do things, and never tell anybody."

Isabel's eyes took a peculiar expression, not wily, not malicious,—but purely secretive.

"I was sorry when she went away," she continued. "But the weather was horrid for two or three months; I don't think the sun shone once. And she couldn't bear it at all, you know. She used to cry all by herself, and I found out that it was because she wanted to see Italy again. So I told mamma that she must go, and mamma sent her all the way back to Sienna. She was a good-natured little woman. I wished her back a hundred times the first week Madame Lepelletier was here."

" Then you too have had a French governess," responded Edith, sympathizingly.

" Oh, yes. How I did dislike her! She was a long, lean, grasshopperish person, with a flat forehead, and a red nose. She was a Protestant, and she called herself very pious. It was so dismal ! She made me learn the History of the Crusade against the Albigenses by heart; and she gave me, for light reading, the Siege of La Rochelle, and the Massacre of St. Bartholomew. They made me perfectly blue. I was very sorry for the poor people, but I couldn't do them any good, you know. And then, just as if it wasn't enough to be advising and lecturing me all day, she used to pester me to death with little notes, telling me of the interest she took in my soul, and full of texts. I got perfectly sick of the sight of them. But at length what do you think she did? She told me a positive, direct, downright fib! I went to mamma, and told her that I would never speak to Madame Lepelletier again, and that the sooner she went away the better."

" Did you really say that to Lady Tremyss?" responded Edith, astonished. " What did she answer?"

" Mamma? Why she said ' very well.' She always says ' very well.' And of course Madame Lepelletier went. I danced about like a Judy for an hour after the carriage drove away; then I burnt up the Albigenses and the Huguenots and La Rochelle, and I burnt up the writing table too. They set the chimney on fire. The men had to climb on the roof, and pour buckets of water down to put it out."

" But wasn't your mamma very much vexed?"

" Mamma never is vexed. She didn't sav

anything to me.    She only told the servants to have the fire put out."

" And was that your last governess?" enquired Edith, who began to take a certain interest in the history of Isabel's duennas.

" No, the next was a German.    Mamma had to get foreigners, for the only way I can learn languages is by hearing people speak.    I can't learn from books; it makes me miserable to study.    As soon as I'm put down to a book it is all I can do to keep myself from running away into the Chase.    Did you ever see the Chase?"

Her eyes sparkled.

" No."

" Oh, it's such a place !    Great trees, full of squirrels ; and if you climb up and sit close and wait, by-and-by very like you'll see a great stately deer, or a little frightened do.. come past.    I have often sat there for hours watching for them."

" But the German governess," suggested Edith, to whom the idea of climbing a great tree and sitting in the branches for hours waiting for the sight of a deer, presented but moderate attractions.

" Yes," answered Isabel, recalling her thoughts from the Chase. " She was a white, puffy-faced woman, with such thick ankles, always calling me 'liebe Fraulein,' and telling me what a rich inner being I had. I never knew what she was talking about. She used to harangue me by the hour about the arts, and the craft of nature, as she called it; and then she would jump plump down from the clouds, and eat cheese, and herrings, and ham,—she said that anything else for luncheon disagreed with her. But she played the piano-forte beautifully. After a while I thought I had better come to an understanding with her, so I said· 'Mademoiselle, I don't like you, and I don't believe that you like me. But I want to play, and you can teach me, so I mean you shall stay here two years; then I shall be sixteen, and I don't intend to have any more governesses after that. Only, there's one thing,—you are not to call me "liebe Fraulein" any more, and I won't hear another word about anything that I can't see or touch.'    You should have seen her face when I began, but by the time I got through, she looked quite contented.    'Wie sie wollen, Fraulein,' she said, and from that time we got on very well together.—But what's Mimi about?" she exclaimed, interrupting her narration.    She directed Edith's attention to where a great Spanish cat was crouching beside a cavity whence some plant had recently been removed.    The creature was peering over the brink; the slight but rapid vibration of its tail showed that it was about to pounce upon some unseen object within.

"She has found a field mouse, I fancy."

Isabel bent eagerly forward, as the cat sprang into the hole.

"I hope not; they are such pretty, harmless little things," said Edith, pitifully. "But no, that is not a field mouse, it is a mole," she exclaimed, as the cat reappeared, triumphantly holding her struggling prey. "Oh, the poor creature."

"But moles aren't harmless things at all," objected Isabel. "They are as cruel and fierce as they can be. If one mole meets another which has anything that he wants, in their underground ways, he will fight with him and kill him to get it. You needn't pity the mole at all."

"But I do," returned Edith, indignantly, "and I mean to get him away from her."

And she ran towards the cat, who, having released her game, was affectionately pawing and turning it over, as a preliminary to the still closer acquaintanceship which she meditated.

As Edith, followed by Isabel, sprang towards her, the cat again seized the mole, and rushed down the terrace. Seeing the glass door already mentioned, ajar, she turned abruptly aside and took refuge in the room within. The two girls followed closely, Isabel laughing aloud in high excitement at the chase.

They darted hither and thither through the great dining-room, following the cat's rapid movements; till at last, dropping the mole, the creature sprang through the window, and disappeared.

"There she goes," cried Isabel. "But the mole, where is he?"

The mole had vanished. They looked around in perplexity.

" He didn't get out through the window, I'm almost sure," said Isabel, dubiously.

" There—there," exclaimed Edith, pointing to a rapidly moving object under the thick Turkey carpet. "He has got underneath. How quick he goes, here; before the sideboard."

They threw themselves down beside the spot, and raised the carpet from the oaken floor. Beneath was a dark, wide spreading stain.

" What is it, Isabel?" said Lady Tremyss, in her quiet, impassive voice, entering. As she spoke, her eye fell on the upturned carpet and on the large, dark stain. She pointed with a mute, imperious gesture to the door. Isabel took Edith's hand, and silently drew her away.

When the door had closed, Lady Tremyss threw herself upon her knees beside the spot. She laid her cheek on it, she pressed her lips to it, uttering the while low inarticulate moans like those of some wounded wild creature. Then she replaced the carpet, and rose to her feet. A horrible smile passed slowly over her features. It vanished, leaving them stirless, as was their wont. She turned and left the room.

The paroxysm had been but brief. As the two girls reached the upper landing of the great staircase, they heard Lady Tremyss' even step as she passed through the hall, and re-entered the drawing room.

" What could it have been ? " asked Edith.

" I'm sure I don't know. A wine stain, I suppose. Perhaps I made too much noise; but mamma never thought I made too much noise before."

They proceeded along the gallery.

"This is my room," said Isabel, pausing as they neared the end. "I do wish the maids would keep that door shut," she exclaimed, petulantly seizing the handle of a half-open door beyond.

"Stop, please," said Edith. "I see pictures. If you are willing, I should like to go in."

Isabel threw open the door.

It was a long room, uncarpeted, the ceiling crossed with heavy oaken beams. On one side was a long range of windows; the opposite wall supported paintings. There was nothing else in the apartment, not a chair, not a table, not even a chest.

There is something singularly depressing in the aspect of an uninhabited room, even if no picture on the wall mock the silence around; but the strange, unreal life such presentments possess, by its contrast adds inexpressibly to one's sense of loneliness and desolation. The eyes fastened full upon you, and from which, shift your position as you will, you cannot get away; the lips, with

their eternal reticence, that yet look ready at each
instant to accost you ; the hands once, doubtless,
busy enough for good or evil, now hanging or
folded in unchanging repose ; the haunting
presence, the dogging footsteps of the past which
press upon you, closely following down the long
vista of some unfrequented gallery; all these
might well influence less impressionable nerves
than those of Edith ; yet, side by side with the
repulsion, stood the fascination such places un-
accountably possess ; it drew her across the
threshold, and lured her on.

The pictures were, for the most part, portraits.
From their apparent antiquity they must have
belonged to the remote ancestry of the family.
Either there was something in the effect of the
grey light which fell from the cloudy sky that
gave a melancholy and severe aspect to the line
of pictured faces, or else the character of the
originals had been singularly forbidding ; but as
Edith passed slowly along their rank, she thought
she had never beheld such stern and menacing

countenances as those that were looking down on her.

"I hate to come into this room," said Isabel, glancing askance at the portraits. "They all look at me as if they hated me; I'm sure I don't know why. I never did them any harm. Come, do let us go back."

"One instant," replied Edith, who at that moment perceived at one end of the gallery a much newer picture than the rest, conspicuous in its gilded frame.

She quickened her steps, and took her stand before it.

It was the portrait of a man somewhat past middle age, short, thickset, powerful. The bull neck, the broad shoulders, the sombre brow, the heavy features, were but partially redeemed by the piercing glance of the eye, and the massive character of the forehead. The fresh colouring of the picture imparted to it a startling life-likeness, seen as it was in contrast with the dim and sunken tones of the paintings around.

"That's Sir Ralph," said Isabel, turning away her head.

"But you do not look like him in the least," remarked Edith.

"I hope not. There's no reason that I should."

"But," questioned Edith, much perplexed, "Is not Lady Tremyss your own mother?"

"Of course, but mamma was married twice. Her first husband was Captain Hartley. After he died she married Sir Ralph."

"Was he kind to you?" asked Edith with a distrustful glance at the scowling brow and Cyclopean shoulders.

"He hadn't much chance to be otherwise. I never came in his way if I could help it. J always hated him. Fortunately, it was easy to keep out of the way, the house is so large.—But do come to my room; we can talk there just as well."

And Isabel hurried Edith up the gallery, carefully closing the door behind them, as if to effectually keep Sir Ralph in.

"Here it is pleasanter, isn't it? I had it all

done to please myself," she said, ushering
Edith into a gaily painted and papered room.

A cultivated taste might have been somewhat disturbed by the irregular and capricious
juxtaposition of the colours employed, and by
their too vivid tone ; yet they seemed, in their
own way, to harmonize with Isabel's style of
beauty. If her surroundings were rather gorgeous, they were certainly becoming. They had
obviously been chosen by instinct, for Isabel had
to all appearance never plunged into the mysteries
of the counter point of colour.

" It looks very bright and cheerful," replied
Edith, as she seated herself on the low chair
which Isabel drew forward. "And now, please
tell me something about your father."

" Yes," returned Isabel, " only first let me
make myself comfortable."

She cast herself full length on the ground,
and crossed her arms over her head. " I love to
lie so. Did you ever try it ?"

" No," said Edith. " It would make me ache

all over.—But you were going to tell me about your father."

" I don't know much, for mamma never speaks of him.   She keeps a miniature of him locked up in her room.   I got a sight of it once when she didn't know.   I look just like him.   I held it up beside my face before the glass to see.   It's older,  and  the features are  larger  and  it  has whiskers, but except that we're just the same."

" How  sad  that  he  should  have  died," said Edith,  gazing down on the beautiful face before her, so full of the joy of life.

" Yes ; I suppose so.   I don't know anything about it.   Let's talk of something else.   Do you ride ? "

" Sometimes."

" Don't you  love  it ? "  asked  Isabel, raising herself on her elbow.   " I should like to live on horseback."

" I was thrown and hurt once, and  that makes me afraid."

" What, have you given it up ? "

" No, I said I rode sometimes. I have been out every day since I came to the Hall on a pony ; but it's lame how."

" What a pity ! " said Isabel, sinking back, with a look of profound commiseration. Then suddenly starting up—" I know what I'll do," she cried, dragging Edith impetuously along the corridor and down the staircase.

" Mamma," she exclaimed, flinging open the drawing-room door, " Miss Arden's pony is lame, and she's afraid of horses, and I want to lend her Moira ; can't I ?"

" Of course," replied Lady Tremyss, raising her eyes an instant, then lowering them again upon her embroidery frame.

" Yes ; but, mamma, I want you to come to the paddock, please. Moira is so fond of you. I want Edith to see."

Lady Tremyss rose, and passing through the hall, took her way along the terrace, followed by Edith and Isabel. As they came to the dining-room window, Isabel's roving eye rested on the

mole lying dead beside the steps.    A little trail
of blood showed where he had made his way from
the dining room.

"See, there's the little gentleman in velvet, as
the old song says," she said, pointing him out to
Edith.

Lady Tremyss turned her head.

"It's the mole, mamma.    Mimi caught him,
and we chased her into the dining room to get
him away, and he crept under the carpet.  It was
then you came in."

Lady Tremyss walked quietly on.    She led the
way through Isabel's flower garden to a door in
the high wall beyond.    As she opened it, a small
black Irish horse which was grazing at the extremity of the enclosure, raised its head and
gazed attentively towards them.    As it recognized Lady Tremyss, it gave a plunge, and came
galloping towards her, its long thick mane and
tail flying behind it.    It circled around the
group, whinnying joyfully, then, coming close, it
laid its head on Lady Tremyss' shoulder.

" See," said Isabel to Edith, who looked somewhat apprehensive, as if she feared a similar
friendly demonstration. " She is just like a
dog, and so easy! Come, Moira, I am going
round the paddock to show you off. Down !"

The horse crouched like a dog, and Isabel
seated herself upon its back.

" Around, mavourneen, around,—softly," she
said. The pony rose carefully, and cantered
gently around the paddock with a wave-like
motion.

Edith's eye followed with delight Isabel's
graceful figure and easy movements.

" How beautifully you ride," she remarked, as
Isabel returned to her starting point.

" Oh, but you should see mamma," she exclaimed, springing down. " I'm nothing to
mamma."

Lady Tremyss turned silently, and led the way
to the gate. Leaving the paddock, they went
towards the house.

" Where's the mole," said Isabel, as they

neared the dining room steps. "Mimi, you know."

The mole had disappeared. Mimi couched beside the place where he had lain.

"Please make her go away," said Edith, who shared the feeling, whether of fear or of distrust, that many sensitive natures experience when brought into contact with any variety of the feline race. "I know it's foolish, but I can't bear to have a cat near me."

"What would you do if you saw a tiger, then?" asked Isabel, signifying to Mimi that her presence was not desired.

"I don't know. I never saw one."

"Neither did I, but I mean to. There's going to be such a great show of wild beasts in the town! I've been watching it in the papers ever so long. I know it's horrid to go to such a place, but for all that I mean to do it. I don't exactly know how I shall manage it," she added, meditatively, "but I shall go; I'm dying to see it."

Dismissing the subject, she chatted about other things until Mrs. Arden's return.

" Well, my dear, and how do you like Isabel ?" asked Mrs. Arden, as the carriage rolled down the avenue.

" Very much."

" And Lady Tremyss ?"

" I don't know."

" Poor thing," continued Mrs. Arden, compassionately; " she's had many trials. I don't see how she has lived through them all, I really don't; and drowning is such a dreadful death! People don't look at all as they do in pictures of it, not at all. I used to think it was such a pleasant way of dying, quite sweet, and so easy ; and then there's that beautiful engraving of a dead saint floating on a river, so touching ;—but I read an account of a visit to the Morgue. The man had got in behind where people don't usually go, and, dear me, it was all so different! I felt quite upset for several days after reading it, I did indeed. The poor people

were all screwed up into S's and Z's ; ugh !" And
a timely shudder came to cut short any further
reminiscences of what the man had seen behind
the Morgue.

But Edith's attention had not followed her
aunt in her discursive comments upon Lady
Tremyss' domestic afflictions.    She was busy in
wondering why Isabel had never once  spoken
of Walter.

As the carriage passed the couchant sphinxes
and turned into the road, she looked around her,
and gave a sigh of relief.   She had not seen
Goliath.

Isabel was as good as her word.    The next
day Moira appeared, led by a groom who bore an
affectionate note to Edith, concluding with an
entreaty that she would keep the horse as long as
she liked.

The groom waited until Walter's horse was
brought to the door, and Edith descended.

"I beg pardon, Miss," he said, touching his
hat, as Edith cast a timid glance upon the mare,

" but there isn't no cause to be shy of her. She's as gentle as a lamb, and ten times more intelligenter. If you'd allow me to advise you, Miss, you'll leave your whip at home. You need only speak to her, she'll understand; but as for a whip, she doesn't like it."

" What would she do?" asked Edith, distrustfully.

" Well, Miss, she wouldn't like it; but, as I said, you haven't nothing to think about when you're on her; she'll take good care of you. Good morning, Miss."

Moira seemed aware of the groom's enconiums, and determined to merit them. Exchanging her canter for an amble, she paced gently along beside Walter's high stepping bay, gradually reassuring Edith, until, she forgot to be afraid and began to chat as if she were on the white pony.

They were approaching a farm house, and Edith was delightedly expatiating on the beauty of some little red and white calves which, huddled together in a ferny corner of a field, were looking over the hedge with their large, soft, startled eyes, curiously gazing at the passers by, when a bull-dog rushed from the open gate of the farm yard, and with the detestable instinct which always teaches his race where attack will inflict the keenest distress, made a furious onset upon Moira's shoulders, jumping up as if trying to reach Edith.

Walter flung himself from his horse, but before he could reach the spot, Moira had wheeled so as to bring her hind legs into position, and inflicting two vigorous kicks upon the brute, flung him forcibly against the stone wall.

After assuring himself that Edith's fright had nothing in it alarming, Walter turned from her.

" I'm not afraid to leave you an instant. Moira will stand," he said, glancing at the mare, who, her eyes shining brightly from beneath her heavy front lock, was watching with evident complacency the retreat of her limping, yelping foe. He advanced to the farm yard.

"Farmer Robeson," he said, quietly addressing a shambling, long faced man, who was in a luke-warm manner superintending the erection of a new cow shed, and who had paid no attention to the savage outburst of his dog, "I have warned you three times already about that dog. I now give you another warning. Your lease is out next October; you will do well to look for another farm. Good morning." Without waiting for any reply, young Arden, who acted as agent for his aunt, mounted his horse and proceeded on his way with Edith, leaving his tenant with gaping eyes and open mouth, whence the sentence came slowly dropping—

"The young Squire! Who'ud ha thought it!"

"Who'd have thought it?" repeated Mrs. Robeson, a plump, black eyed, little woman, who came flying from the house into the farm-yard like a bomb shell, and there exploded. "Who'd have thought it? Any body that had two eyes beside their nose, and a head a-top of them, would have thought it. Haven't you been

behindhand with your rent, till anyone else
would have turned you out long ago?" Like
many other women, Mrs. Robeson, on occa-
sions of distressful emergency, invariably
abandoned the customary conjugal plural.
"Haven't I been preaching and preaching,
till I was as hoarse as a young turkey-chick with
the pip, telling you that you had better keep on
the right side of the young Squire, for that he'd
got a wrong one to him, for all so pleasant as
he looks. And now you can do no better than
to bring him here, with his face as white as a
sheet, and his eyes two coals of fire, to tell you
that the lease is out next October. And such
an easy rent! and all the money for repairs and
drainage! and where are you going to find such
grass land again?—Get out of my sight, you cur,"
she exclaimed, the stream of her indignation being
for the moment diverted from its original
direction by the yelps of the cause of the disaster;
and seizing a rake, she drove the offender into
an empty cart room, there to moralize on social

distinctions, whilst awaiting his doom. Then briskly returning to the house, without deigning a glance at her partner, she dressed herself in her best, and picking a bunch of the brightest flowers her garden afforded, and gathering a basket of her finest fruit, she betook herself to the Hall, ensconcing herself in the house-keeper's room, until the time of Edith's return.

"I've looked at her in church, and I'll trust her to make our peace with the young Squire and Madam Arden. She looks as soft as snow, but there's steel has gone to the making of her, I'll warrant."

Nor did Dame Robeson's manner of acquitting herself of her embassy, disgrace her penetration. Having, by Nitson's intermediation, been admitted to an interview with the young lady, she enumerated to Edith the many favours her husband had received from the family; and lamented his thriftlessness and remissness, especially in the matter of the rent.

"He's a regular born innocent, poor man,

Miss," she said;—for dame Robeson exchanged her home trumpet for a flute, when she crossed the domestic threshold. She penitently accused herself as the guilty cause of the dog being retained, giving as her excuse that the farm-house was a lonely one, and that the previous tenant had been saved from the murderous midnight attack of three robbers, solely by the timely interference of a ferocious watch dog; and finally she besought Edith to save them from the double misfortune of losing at once so advantageous a lease and so good a landlord; "for Miss," she concluded, "it is not for the like of me to be praising my betters, but I say no more than all the parish says, when I say that there isn't a gentleman in the whole county that can stand beside our young Squire."

And Edith, her sympathies strongly excited by Mrs. Robeson's manner of stating her case, promised to speak in farmer Robeson's behalf.

The subject was under discussion as she entered the drawing-room before dinner.

"I never liked Robeson, never liked him at all," Mrs. Arden was saying. "I'm glad he is going, I'd rather have him off the estate than on it. I don't care so much about his not paying his rent, but when it's got so that people can't be sure of their lives passing his gate, I say it's time he was gone," she ended; her habitual benevolence quite over balanced for the moment, by the ascendency of her timidity. To her imagination, excited as it had been by the account of the creature's attack upon Edith, the bull-dog stood four feet five in his toes, and was of corresponding dimensions. "No, I'm determined he shall go the day his lease is out, and you did quite right to tell him so."

The moment was unpropitious : Edith must wait. But she had not to wait long ; the wished for opportunity soon presented itself.

"How much stronger you have grown," said Walter, as they sat over the chess table after dinner, slowly arranging the pieces. He con-

templated with satisfaction the rounding outlines
of her figure, and the delicate pink of her cheek.
"I am sure that fright would have knocked you
up a little while ago."

" Do you know I like that Roman Catholic
custom of acts of gratitude," responded Edith,
without any very obvious reference to her cousin's
remark.

" What are they ?  I never heard of them."

" When one has some great good to be thankful for, they do something to make others happy.
Is it not a good practice ? "

" Yes, that's all right."

" Then will you help me ? " she asked, with
one of her smiles.

" But you must first tell me what your act of
gratitude is to give thanks for?"

" It is for being brought here," she answered,
simply.

As she met the earnest, unconsciously searching
glance he fastened upon her, a blush rose on

Edith's cheek, a blush that comes but once; the blush of the young girl who feels for the first time that she is no longer a child.

A something, he knew not what, almost painful in its sweetness, thrilled Walter from head to foot.

—Was that blush for him?—

"Ask me anything," he said.

"Let farmer Robeson stay."

"Anything."

\*          \*          \*          \*

The adventure of the bull-dog had probably somewhat shaken Edith's nerves, for she awoke from her next morning's slumber with a piercing shriek, much to the alarm of Nitson, who was sewing at the window. She dropped her scissors, upset her work-basket, and sprang forward.

"Oh! gracious me, Miss, you've had a bad dream."

"Yes," replied Edith, glancing around with an expression of relief. "I dreamed that Sir

Ralph's portrait was trying to get out of the picture gallery, and that Miss Hartley and I were holding the door against it. Oh! there it is again!" she exclaimed, as a loud clap came from without.

" Dear me, Miss, that's only a blind on the next story that has got loose. The wind is rather high this morning."

" What a face Sir Ralph's is," said Edith uneasily, half to herself. " I wish I had not seen it."

" Oh, but Miss, you must not let a picture that's nothing but a picture get on your nerves. Sir Ralph wasn't a bad sort of a gentleman, for all that he was rather ill-favoured. My third cousin by the mother's side was housekeeper at the Park till she died, last year, of an annyeurism, the doctors said it was; and I've spent many an hour there, and knew all the ongoings of the house as well as if I lived there. Sir Ralph just fairly doated on my lady. To be sure, he never wanted her to speak to any-

body  se, and he was even jealous-like of **Miss**
Hartley, but **that was** all along of his great love
for her.   He'd have given her the eyes **out of his**
head.   **Why,** that very horse you rode yesterday,
Miss, Sir Ralph paid **four** hundred guineas **for it.**
Not that it was worth it, for it wasn't.   I've
heard the coachman **say** its value wasn't much
except for the tricks it can do, for it was trained
like a dog ;—and that's only one thing out of
many."

" You say he was jealous of Miss Hartley?"
asked Edith.

" Oh, yes, Miss !" replied **Nitson,** much pleased
at the unwonted liberty her tongue was allowed.
" I'm sorry to say there wasn't no doubt about
that.   The servants said he would scowl if he
did but hear her voice.   It might have frightened
another child, but she was as bold as a little
lion.   She never went near him, to be sure, but
that wasn't because she was afraid of him.   Once
I was in the housekeeper's room, and she was
running through the long entry, and she met Sir

Ralph.    That entry was like a sort of whispering gallery, you could hear anything that was said in it from one end to the other.    They stopped for a moment.    I suppose he looked at her some way she did not like, for the next minute I heard her say 'I hate you, Sir Ralph,' and off she ran. I expect his conscience pricked him for his dislike of her, for I heard him mutter, 'she's right.' "

"And Goliath?" questioned Edith, turning on her side, and looking inquiringly at Nitson. "Then you know something about him."

"Oh, Miss, there's a man!    If ever there was a good Christian on this earth, it's Mr. Goliath, for all his black skin—not that his skin goes against it, for I've heard that one of the chiefest fathers of the church, as they call them, was a black man.    But as for Mr. Goliath, for long suffering and patient mindedness, he is a crown of glory."    Nitson's images when she was excited on any topic, were apt to become obscure. "Why, Miss, the day Sir Ralph threw the decanter at him, and cut open his face, and it's a mercy he

didn't make him blind of an eye for life—that very
day when Mrs. Pralyn, that was the housekeeper that
was my cousin, was staunching the wound, for it
bled most fearful, and binding it up, she couldn't
help saying something **sharp** about Sir **Ralph**.
She told me she couldn't keep her tongue **between**
her teeth for that once, for all that she was a prudent
woman that didn't look **upon herself as** justified
in bearing any witness against **her** masters.
And what do you think Mr. Goliath answered,
Miss? He said Sir Ralph was **hot in his** temper
always, **but that** it was nothing **to think** about.
Sir Ralph would feel sorry some day. My cousin,
Mrs. Praylin, the housekeeper, said **that she**
looked at him as **he spoke, and at** that very
moment, **what with the pain** and the natural
grief he felt at receiving such a hurt, his face was
quite a pale greenish colour, instead of being black
as it always was before and after. **And he might**
well take it **to heart, Miss,** for though it's **hard to**
believe now that he **has got that awful scar, he**
**used to be one of the handsomest men I ever**

looked on, in spite of his colour, and now there isn't nobody that can brook the sight of him scarcely. Some wonder why Lady Tremyss keeps him in such a place, but he's been in the family a long time, and the scar is none of his fault. But, Miss, I'm tiring you, I expect, and that before you are out of your bed."

And Nitson actively commenced the preparations for Edith's toilette.

Edith would gladly have questioned her about Lady Tremyss, but her disinclination to hear more of Nitson's gossip overcame her curiosity, and she finished dressing, and left the room without any further conversation with her maid.

Her dream, and Nitson's commentary, faded from her mind as she descended the staircase, and her thoughts reverted to her embarrassment of the previous evening. As she entered the breakfast-room, the flush that haunted her memory re-appeared upon her cheeks. It was only as the breakfast proceeded that she at length became at ease. He talked just as usual. He certainly had not noticed it.

And all the time before Walter's eyes floated the rosy light of Edith's blush.

The day was fine. The horses came to the door, Moira still officiating in place of the little white pony, and Edith and Walter took their way through the avenue, and past the rounding hollows of the Meadland farm.

As they turned their horses into a narrow and unfrequented lane, in which Walter assured her she would find any quantity of eglantine, they perceived at a little distance, a man walking from them. There was an air of dejection and neglect about him, that scarcely warranted by his powerful frame.

Moira suddenly quickened her pace, and pressing close to the man, thrust her nose into his hand. He looked round quickly.

" Is it you, old girl—is it you?" he said. " I might have known you weren't a human, to be so friendly." Then raising his eyes, he touched his hat to Walter. " Beg pardon, Sir ; but you saw it was none of my fault. I always took care of her, and she remembers."

He patted Moira's neck.

" I am sorry to see you in such a poor plight, George," said young Arden, disapproval and compassion struggling in his tone.

" Thank you, Sir. I never thought to see myself like this."

The man glanced at his tattered sleeve.

" I should have thought so good a groom as you are would have been able to find a place."

" Ah, Sir ! you know the proverb about giving a dog a bad name. It's worse for a man. I've found places enough, and all seemed straight until they asked the name of my last master. And that was the end of it; for you know, Sir, it was all in the papers how—" The man stopped a moment.—" I did get a place with a horse breaker; but, Sir, it's hard when you've lived under gentlemen all your life, to take orders from them as aren't gentlemen. I had good wages, and I understood the work, but I wasn't contented, Sir. I gave it up, and tried again to get into a gentleman's stables; but it wasn't of no use."

"What brought you back to this part of the country? You surely must have known that your chance was better elsewhere."

"Well, Sir—I may as well say it—there was a young woman, Sir—" His face twitched. "But there's no use in speaking of that, Sir. It is all over, and I don't blame her."

There was something in the man's utter dejection and unresenting hopelessness that pained Edith to the quick. She averted her eyes, though she sat where he could not see her.

"It is hard on you, George, I acknowledge, very hard, that one single instance—for I believe it was the only time—"

"The only time, Sir, in all my life. I never liked drink. I never wanted it. And all along of one glass of wine."

"How's that?" enquired Walter, somewhat distrustfully.

"So sure as God Almighty is above us, Mr. Arden, I never touched a drop of anything that day, except a pint of ale and one glass of wine."

"How came you to be drinking wine?"

Young Arden did not like the improbability of the assertion. His voice was growing colder.

"It was Mr. Goliath, Sir. Just before Sir Ralph started, Mr. Goliath called me into the pantry, and told me that my lady was very uneasy because my master was going to ride Kathleen. He told me to keep a good look-out, and see that no harm came of it; and he poured me out a glass of port wine, and I drank it. I didn't like the taste of it much, but I had never tasted any before; and, Sir, it got into my head. I began to feel queer while I was riding, but the air kept it off awhile. When we got there and I went into the servants' hall, I couldn't hold my head up. I sat down in a window-seat, and never spoke a word. They said I was asleep; but I wasn't, Sir. I was looking at faces all the time."

"What do you mean, George?" said young Arden. "Looking at faces!"

"Looking at faces, Sir," the man repeated, firmly. "I saw them plainer than I see you now." He fixed his haggard eyes on the young gentleman. "I thought I was in a sort of tool-house, whitewashed, with black patches here and there, where the whitewash had peeled off, and so long that I didn't see the end of it. And there were people—a whole procession of them—that never stopped; and they stared at me as they went by; and their faces were so thin, and so white, and so starved-looking, and some of them looked so wicked, Sir, that I'd have looked away, only I couldn't. At last some one came and told me as how the gentlemen were going. I got up, and some of the other grooms helped me to get my master's and my own horse ready; but they'd no sooner got me into my saddle than I fell off, and after that I didn't know anything till they woke me up next morning—for I stayed in the barn all night on the hay—telling me that Sir Ralph was drownded, and all along of me."

"This is a strange story, George," said young Arden, doubtfully; "a very strange story. I never heard of a man's being intoxicated by a single glass of wine."

The man made no reply.

Edith bent forward.

"Walter, I believe every word he has said."

"God bless you, Miss," burst from the man's lips.

"I've watched him, and he is telling the truth."

Walter looked at her a moment. A kindred conviction was beginning to communicate itself to his mind.

"I can't stop longer now," he said to the groom, "but come to the Hall to-morrow morning. I'll see what can be done."

Slipping a piece of money into the man's reluctant hand, he rode on with Edith.

" I don't understand the thing at all," he said, ponderingly. " A single glass of wine? It sounds like a bare-faced falsehood."

" I don't judge people by facts,"—Edith remarked.

" No ?" said her cousin. "By what do you judge them then ?"

" I judge them by their faces. Faces never deceive, but facts may ; I mean what we think facts, may."

" And are you never deceived in faces ?"

" I sometimes meet faces that I cannot understand—Lady Tremyss' for instance; but I never make up my mind and find afterwards that I have been mistaken."

" You know we men aren't so sharp witted as women in that way. We have nothing but facts to go by."

" What are you going to do for that poor

man ?"—interrupted Edith, aware, that in spite of facts, the groom's cause was gained.

" I'm sure I don't know. It's very awkward. I can't take him myself, because of Lady Tremyss."

" No, you could not do that, and he would not be happy ; you remember what—"

Edith paused.

" Poor fellow ! I pity him from the bottom of my heart," said Walter, his natural benevolence now in full ascendency.

He rode on for a while in silence, then, abruptly turning to Edith, said :

" What do you think of sending him out to Canada ? He would have a new chance there."

" I think it would be just the thing," she exclaimed eagerly, " the very best thing. All the disgrace and pain would lie behind him, and he would still be among his own people. I think it an admirable idea. I wish he could know it now."

" Would you like to turn back and tell him ?" asked Walter, drawing his rein. " He has not gone far."

" Oh, no, I am not quite so impatient as that. It would be better to have everything settled and arranged, and to look in the paper to see when the next vessel sails, and to tell him everything at once. We will wait till to-morrow morning."

On reaching the Hall they found Mrs. Arden in a state of excitement, Nitson having reported Letty Prast as crying her eyes out and refusing to say why.

" What has distressed Letty so much?" asked Edith.

" It's all about a man, and a very bad man, I'm sorry to say. It's that groom of Sir Ralph's. It seems they used to be fond of each other when she was in service at the Park, and she had set her heart on him, and they were to have been married as soon as they had saved up a little money; and I declare I can't help being sorry for her, I can't indeed, for it wasn't her fault, you know. Then all that happened, and her mother made her promise never to have anything more to say to him; and now he's come back, and I'm afraid he got a sight of her last night, for she's done nothing but cry ever since. She'd have cried a great deal more if she had married him, and so I told Nitson, and Nitson said that she'd told her so, and said all the other comforting things to her that she could think of; but that at all she said she only cried the more."

Leaving Walter to explain as much of George's story as he thought proper, Edith proceeded through the offices until she reached the laundry.

Her knock, for she did not wish to take the girl by surprise, was answered by a stifled " Come in."

Letty stood diligently ironing a damask table cloth. She did not raise her head at Edith's entrance. The young lady stood for a moment uncertain how to begin. The presence of a great grief will check the expression of the kindliest sympathy. Letty continued her occupation in silence. At last Edith spoke.

" I have heard, Letty—I have come to tell you how sorry I am."

" Thank you, Miss," Letty answered, and went on with her ironing. Anyone might have thought the girl devoid of feeling were it not for the beating of the vein in her throat.

Edith bent over the ironing table.

" I have seen him, seen him this morning, and I do not believe he has done anything wrong."

Letty dropped her iron, sat down, covered her head with her apron and began to cry bitterly.

" It is very hard, very hard indeed, that he should be innocent, and that every one should believe him guilty," Edith continued.

" Not me, Miss, I never thought him guilty, never, never, oh! never," sobbed Letty from under her apron.

" Mr. Arden is going to try to get him a place with a friend of his, and I am sure you will not be sorry to have him go where he can begin life afresh;"—Letty made a movement of attention—

" He is going to ask this gentleman to take George with him to Canada ."

A suppressed exclamation came from under the apron.

" It seems a long way off, I know, but he will soon be there, and then he will have no one to bring up all these stories against him, and he will be like a new man ; and bye-and-bye he will come back, or, perhaps, you might go out to him."

Letty burst afresh into weeping.

" Oh, Miss ! I promised my mother, and I can't. I would now if it wasn't for that, and I told him so last night; but I cannot break my promise. I wish I hadn't made it; but it's too late now—it's too late."

" Don't say too late," urged Edith. " I can't think that anything so dreadful as the innocent being thought guilty can go on for ever. Don't cry, Letty, take heart, and believe that better days are coming." And after encouraging and

comforting Letty to the best of her ability, finding it difficult to maintain a conversation which
consisted solely of exhortations on the one side,
and sobs on the other, Edith left the laundry to
confer anew with Walter.

The next morning no George appeared at the
Hall.   A poor woman came to say that he could
not move from his bed.   Edith had the woman
brought into the hall, and went out to see her.

"He's dreadful bad, Miss,—tooked with the
rheumatiz all over.   He can't move no more nor
his hand, poor soul, and he's all of a live coal with
the fever.   He said he couldn't no ways bear
that the young Squire and the Miss should think
ill of him, for not coming up, so I just made
bold to come up myself, Miss."

Further questions elicited the cause of George's
illness : he had slept for the three preceding
nights under hedges.

Mrs. Arden effervesced into active benevolence
forthwith, and ordered a basket to be made ready
with all the comforts the occasion required.   She

would gladly have gone down herself, but Walter protested, and despatched a groom for Dr. Frintly, dismissing the woman with Mrs. Arden's basket, and a message that he would call himself in the course of the day.

"I think Letty had better not hear anything about it," said Mrs. Arden, returning to the parlour. "I've told Wiggins not to say a word about it. She couldn't go down to take care of him, you know, and this Dingall seems a nice sort of a woman, and will take good care of him, I've no doubt, very good care indeed: it would only make the girl more miserable to hear about it, and, from what Nitson says, she's bad enough now, quite bad enough, so she is not to know anything." A decision which appeared the best practicable, and which was accordingly adhered to.

When Walter called that afternoon at Mrs. Dingall's cottage, he found the man in a stupor.

"He's been so, Sir, pretty nearly ever since he took the doctor's stuff," said the woman.

"He was in dreadful pain before; but he quieted down very soon, and hasn't taken notice of anything since."

The stupor went off before the evening, and when Doctor Frintly called again at eight o'clock, he found his patient awake.

"Well, my man, how's the pain?" he said, cheerfully, as he entered the little attic; skilfully avoiding bringing his head in contact with the low, slanting roof, while he advanced to the bed side.

"The pain is easier, Sir, thank you; but please, Sir, for God's sake, don't never give me no more port wine."

"Port wine," repeated the doctor, darting a scrutinizing glance at his face. "Who's been giving you port wine?"

"Mrs. Dingall, Sir. She brought it from the apothecary's."

"Mrs. Dingall didn't know what she was talking about when she called it port wine. It was an anodyne."

" It wasn't she, Sir. I've tasted it before, and what I had this morning was port wine."

" Hope he isn't out of his head," thought the doctor, feeling his patient's pulse. The anodyne had certainly not produced the effect he had anticipated. The man's pulse was higher, his eye was restless, his nerves were obviously much excited.

" Where was it that you drank port wine?" he questioned, carefully examining the man's countenance as he spoke.

" In the pantry at the Park, Sir."

" Well, if you drank it there, you drank precious good wine, I can tell you. Sir Ralph's cellar was the best in the county."

" This was just like it, Sir."

" He's not out of his head," thought Dr. Frintly, as the result of his investigation. " What the devil can he be talking about?"

" How did it taste?"

" Queerish, Sir."

" Queerish. A good many things taste queerish beside port wine."

" It wasn't only the taste, Sir, it was how it made me feel."

" How did it make you feel?"

" Most dreadful, Sir."

" Well, but how?"

" I'd rather not say, Sir, please; I don't like to think about it," said George, glancing uneasily around.

" He tells a straight story enough—puzzling enough, too," thought the doctor. " It may be that port wine disagrees with him—sherry does with some people; but it wasn't port wine.—Can it be that that rascally Barrows has sent him port wine instead of the anodyne! I'll see."

Giving a few directions to the woman, and writing a new prescription, he got into his gig, and drove to the apothecary's shop.

His knocks, vigorous as they were, sounded but faintly to the ears of Mr. Barrows, who, in the little inner room, stretched upon two chairs, was holding a bottle of chloroform to his nose.

" That's some one knocking," he said at length,

meditatively, to himself; but it required a whole volley of subsequent peals to rouse him from his recumbent position, and bring him to the door.

He opened it, then, with a swaying motion, retreated behind the counter, where he stood under the dim light of the smoky lamp, supporting himself upon both hands.

" Well, Barrows, you've kept me long enough hammering there. What were you about? Taking a nap, I'll be bound."

Mr. Barrows went through a mental calculation as to whether he had better say yes or no. He decided in favour of yes, as being most amicable and thereby tending to stave off enquiry.

" Yes, sir."

Dr. Frintly turned and drew in his breath two or three times through his nostrils, striking terror to the soul of Barrows.

" You've been making up something with chloroform, haven't you?"

" Yes, sir."

There was a very disagreeable ringing in

Barrow's ears. He feared it would tip him over, and held on tighter than ever to the counter.

"Some of Folfrew's stuff, I suppose," continued Dr. Frintly, with a little "whew" of disgust. Dr. Folfrew being a rival practitioner, who had contracted a bad habit of getting in his way.

Mr. Barrow's attention was for the moment absorbed by the rapidly increasing magnitude and brilliancy of Dr. Frintly's gilt waiscoat buttons; but suddenly coming to a perception that he was expected to say something, he answered, "Yes, sir."

"I haven't come to talk about his tom-fool prescriptions. I suppose it's a lotion for some old woman's cat."

Yes, sir, seemed to answer very well. Mr. Barrows thought it prudent to keep to it, so he again replied, "Yes, sir."

Dr. Frintly rubbed his hands together and laughed aloud with a mixture of professional and gladiatorial delight.

"I've guessed it then! I never thought of hitting true. What a capital story against Folfrew."

Dr. Frintly's indignation was for the moment in a fair way of total evaporation in his satisfaction at the idea of what a handle against Folfrew the "Sick cat Lotion" would prove; but a reminiscence of the port wine returning, he all at once changed his tone and addressed Mr. Barrows, who was trying to count the bottles on the opposite shelf by way of steadying his head.

"Now, Barrows, just tell me one thing. Did you give that woman, Dingall, port wine instead of the anodyne this morning?"

Barrows attempted to repeat the question to himself, but the words faded into thin air. The only fact that he was conscious of was that a face which had suddenly become ireful, was looking at him, expecting an answer. "No," might lead to further questions, and what were the questions about? From out the cloud of his mental faculties the hapless Barrows again meekly uttered,

" Yes, sir."

" And what in the devil's name did you do that for?" vociferated Dr. Frintly, giving a blow with his fist on the edge of the desk, which jarred everything around. " Do you know that if you'd made the mistake the other way you might have killed somebody?"

Barrows closed his eyes and tried to think what it was all about.

" Pretty mess you might have made of it! Where is Witchkins? In bed, I suppose, and long enough he'll stay there unless he gets better care than his own to pull him through. Give him my compliments and tell him that I advise him to get a new assistant."

Barrows, who was by this time impressed with the idea that he was lying on his back behind the counter, and that the upper half of Dr. Frintly's body, minus legs, was floating close to the ceiling directly above him, in a state of terrific indigna-

tion, essayed  one more attempt at propitiation
by means of a feeble, " Yes, Sir."

Dr. Frintly issued from the shop, shutting the
door behind him, with a crash that rattled all the
glass stoppers in the bottles.

## CHAPTER IV.

THE next morning, Edith accompanied Walter to the cottage, and waited at the door, while he made his visit above. Mrs. Dingall, a small, blear eyed woman, with an habitually down-cast expression, came forward in obedience to a sign from Edith.

" Oh, yes, Miss, he's better now, much better, Miss, but he was awful bad the first night. He talked—I don't know whether it was in his sleep or not, he was so queer like, but he talked the whole time about Mr. Goliath, and the river, and Sir Ralph, till I was clean afraid he'd bring Sir Ralph's ghost to hear what it was all about. And, Miss," she added, glancing over her shoulder,

"I'm not sure he didn't, for I heard the shutter move outside the window, I did, Miss, as sure as I'm standing here, and there wasn't a breath of air stirring, Miss, not a single breath. And I heard footsteps, I didn't dare to look out, but I heard footsteps, Miss, and they stopped on the gravel below the window, ever so long a while, and then they went away."

Edith looked up at the window of the attic.

"But, my good woman, nobody is tall enough to reach the window shutter."

She had forgotten the supposed supernatural character of the visitant.

"That's just it, Miss, nobody is tall enough, and it was reached; so you see that proves it was a ghost."

Mrs. Dingall's fears, expanding as is usually the case, by expression, were rapidly becoming convictions.

"But you do not really believe in ghosts," said Edith, contemplating her interlocutor with some curiosity.

"Not believe in 'em, Miss!" repeated the woman, with a look of shocked piety. "I wouldn't dare not to believe in em; and as to Sir Ralph's ghost, it isn't the first time he's come."

"What do you mean?" asked Edith."

"Well, Miss, nobody speaks of it, for my lady was very much displeased when she heard of it; but the night Sir Ralph was drownded, his ghost came and told of it with an awful shout; it woke some of the maids. They were so frighted, Miss, that they didn't dare to move, for all that they thought it sounded like Sir Ralph's voice. And true enough, the next thing they knew, the house was roused, and there was Mr. Goliath, his clothes all dripping, for he'd been uneasy about his master because of the horse he rode, which was so vicious; and he'd been down to look out for him, and had seen it all, and been into the river himself, and Sir Ralph was drownded. And it's all true, Miss. One of the maids is daughter to the woman who lives next to me, in that little cottage there, and it was she that told me ; but she said my lady ordered it to be made known to them, that if any of the household ever spoke of such a story again, they should lose their places; for my lady doesn't believe in ghosts, Miss."

" I don't wonder she was displeased," said Edith, thinking that she herself would greatly resent having a ghost admitted as an imaginary inmate of Arden Court.

Walter's appearance at the door of the cottage interrupted Mrs. Dingall's relation. With a few kindly words and a gratuity to George's nurse he left the cottage.

" How is he this morning?" asked Edith, feeling with a certain sensation of relief as she she looked at him, that young Arden's powerful frame, clear eyes and pleasant smile, disproved the theory of ghosts.

" He's much better; in a few days he'll be up again. He tells me that Frintly says he has just escaped a rheumatic fever. But what do you think?—it's really curious,—Witchkin's stupid assistant sent the poor fellow port wine instead of an anodyne, and it produced the same effect as before."

"How very strange. It seems impossible," replied Edith, doubtingly.

"So I should have said, but Frintly rode over to enquire, and the assistant, careless donkey, owned that he had made the mistake."

"I don't like to have things coincide so," said Edith, after a pause. "It does not seem natural."

"The chief thing is, after all, that he is better, you know," returned young Arden, "and happy enough at the idea of going away."

"Yes, please tell me about that," said Edith.

"It seemed a great relief to him. He has been dogged by ill-luck so long that at first he was scarcely able to believe he was at length to have a fair chance, like any other man. I wish I could get him a place as groom there. I would rather that he had everything clear before him when he sails."

" But do you know any one in Canada?" questioned Edith.

"Not a soul.   The only way would be to get him a place with some one going out."   Walter pondered a while, then exclaimed,

"I have it.   There's Frank Daubenay; his regiment is just ordered there.   I'll write to him by this very mail.   It would be a capital berth for George.   Daubenay is the kindest-hearted fellow in existence."

" I think, Aunt, I shall be able to get George a place as groom, with Daubenay," said Walter, at lunch.   "You know a first-rate English groom is not easily found willing to leave England, and he'll be wanting one there."

" Is a Daubenay really going out to Canada?" inquired Mrs. Arden, her eyes looking very large.

"Yes ; Daubenay's regiment was ordered off last week."

"Dear me, how very strange that is," said Mrs. Arden.   " And yet it would be awkward to exchange under the circumstances, perhaps."

"What circumstances?" asked Walter. "It's not such very hard duty in Canada. Plenty of pretty girls, and balls by the dozen. But why shouldn't he go?"

"Dear me, didn't you ever hear of it? Why, I thought everybody had heard of it. Such a noise as it made, and everybody taking sides for or against. I never knew what to believe about it. All I was sure of was that it was a dreadful thing, and that the poor young man was very much to be pitied all the same, whether he were right or wrong, you know."

"But I don't know," said Walter; "that's precisely what I want you to tell me."

"Well, then, Frank Daubenay's uncle, Henry Daubenay, was condemned to death in Canada," responded Mrs. Arden, emphatically.

"A gentleman! How dreadful!" exclaimed Edith.

"Yes; wasn't it perfectly shocking? It quite broke his father's heart—quite. He never held up his head afterwards, but took to his bed and died, poor man."

" I never heard anything of this," said Walter.
" How was it?   It is hard on Daubenay."

" It was all because of some dreadful colonel.
He told Daubenay to do something or other, and
Daubenay wouldn't, and they quarrelled, and
Daubenay drew his sword on him—I'm quite cer-
tain about that—and so he was condemned by a
court-martial."

" And was he executed?" asked Edith, in a
low voice.

" No, dear; oh, no.   It was very bad, but not
quite so bad as that.   The day before he was to
have been shot, he escaped.   I was so glad when
the news came.   It was his wife who got him off,
so everybody thought, for she disappeared at the
same time.   He'd been married only a little
while to Lady Emily Blackland.   She had run
away and followed him out to Canada."

" Why couldn't she marry him here?" asked
Edith.

" Her parents opposed it, for he was a very
wild young man, my dear."

" And what became of them?" inquired Edith.

" Nobody knew, my dear, and it was a great deal better they shouldn't, for if he had ever been found again, he would have been shot. People thought they had made their way to the States, poor things.—But come, Edith, you must go and lie down on the sofa; you know Lady Tremyss and Isabel dine here to-day. I do hope Isabel will be quiet and sit still. I'd as lief have a salamander in the room when she's in one of her wild moods ; I had, indeed."

When Edith entered her room to dress for dinner, she found an evening toilette of white muslin and Valenciennes displayed on the bed.

" Oh, no; please give me a high dress," she said to Nitson, who stood complacently surveying the delicate material and costly trimming.

Nitson's face fell.

" Certainly, Miss, if you say so," she answered, moving towards the wardrobe. " Only Lady Tremyss keeps very strict to London ways, and she and Miss Hartley are always low-necked in the evening; and so I thought, Miss, perhaps it would be pleasanter for them if you were low-necked, too. But it's just as you say," she concluded, with treacherous submission, opening the wardrobe door.

Thus presented in the light of a duty, Edith assumed the dress; but looked with distrust upon the parure of turquoise which Nitson produced.

"No, Nitson; really that is too much."

"If you think so, Miss. Only Miss Hartley always wears ornaments, and I thought it would please Mrs. Arden to see you looking nice."

Assailed on a second vulnerable point, Edith yielded.

As Nitson gave the last skilful touches to Edith's showery golden curls, her heart swelled with the majestic pride of the successful lady's maid.

"There now!" she soliloquised, looking after Edith, as she left the room, "I wonder who'll say now that Miss Hartley is handsomer than my young lady! Not but what Miss Hartley is beautiful to look at, there's no denying that; but somehow, she's like running water—it's flash, flash, flash, all the time. But Miss Arden, she's just like the pond on the top of Llangwir,—you can look down and down into it. How lovely she does look in that muslin and Valenciennes, to be sure. I'll go and tell Mrs. Pomfret to put herself where she'll get a peep at her."

"Come nearer, my dear," said Mrs. Arden, looking up from her novel, as Edith appeared in the drawing-room. "I want to look at you. Dear me, how very nice!"

She touched caressingly her niece's soft, floating curls.

"I'm afraid I'm too much dressed," said Edith, a little apprehensively; "but Nitson seemed quite sure."

Whatever Mrs. Arden ventured to think, she only replied—

"You look very nice, my dear, very nice, indeed. I think Adeline Crane, in this book, must have looked very much as you do now; only I hope the likeness won't go any further, I'm sure, for she had three husbands, all at a time, and yet she seems to have been a nice sort of person, too."

Mrs. Arden returned to her novel, while Edith retired to a sofa, and worked at some purple and silver crotchet work, until Lady Tremyss and Miss Hartley were announced. At the same instant Walter entered, and almost directly the doors of the dining-room were thrown open; so that Edith was not able fairly to look at Lady Tremyss and her daughter until they were all seated at the table.

Under the lamplight their peculiar and strongly contrasted beauty assumed new vividness. Lady Tremyss' purely cut features, her length of sable hair, braided and wound around the back of her head, displaying its severely classic outline, her colourless complexion, the exquisite modelling of her neck and arms, relieved against her dress of black lustreless silk, gave her the appearance of some priestess on an Etruscan vase; while her intent look, even when listening and replying to the veriest trifles, the unslumbering expression of her eye, communicated something incomprehensible to her presence. Edith felt she stood before that which was entirely out of the scope of her perceptions.—What was Lady Tremyss' ruling motive,—she began to ask herself.—By what tie was she bound to life?—She was still pondering, when Isabel spoke to her mother. As Lady Tremyss turned her eyes upon her daughter, they softened momentarily, then became cold and inscrutable as before. One look, and yet it was enough. Edith felt that she had solved the mystery. That instant had illumined to her view the sealed recesses of Lady Tremyss' heart.

"Nor is it strange," she thought, directing her attention to Isabel, who with heightened colour and brilliant eyes, was dilating to Walter upon the qualities of some music by a new composer.

Isabel was, as Nitson had predicted, in full dinner costume. Her white dress and sash were em-

broidered with small crimson flowers, a spray of
fuchsia was placed among the waving masses of her
brown hair, and about her slender throat was
twisted a glittering snake of black enamel and gold.
Her fingers were loaded with rings, which shed a
shower of sparks with every motion of her hands.
There was a provoking grace, an elf-like spor-
tiveness, a flush and glow of unquiet life about
her, that made her all but intoxicating to look
upon.   You were pleased, you were vexed, you
were delighted, you were piqued, all at once, and
you could not tell why.

"Does Walter feel it?   He must;" thought
Edith, glancing shyly at her cousin.

A brighter flush rose on her cheek, a faint
smile deepened the corners of her mouth, as she
dropped her eyes.

Walter was listening with an air more absent
than interested; his eyebrows were imperceptibly
raised, his lips were pressed a trifle closely together.   In fact, Isabel was rather boring him.
She had talked to him so many times before,

just as she was talking then; and he was used, of late, to something so much better.

In spite of her beauty, Isabel was not attractive to Walter. The superficial character of her mind, the trivial nature of her interests, the restless changefulness of her moods, had never been displeasing to young Arden; but since he had known Edith, Isabel's gay prattle had become distasteful to his ear, her sparkling beauty wearied his eye. Something of this Edith felt as she sat there.

—" Walter does not care for Isabel."—She had not yet turned the next page. She had not yet learned to think,—" Walter does care for me." —

Then came the thought—" I hope Isabel does not care for him."—

She turned to her. Isabel's rapid flow of talk had ceased for an instant.

" Let me thank you for all the pleasure you have given me," said Edith. " You do not know how I have enjoyed these rides. I shall send

Moira back to-morrow; the pony must be well by this time."

Isabel laughed.

"You can't be sure." And, turning to young Arden, she asked archly, "Walter, is the pony well?"

"I don't know that it is," returned Walter, conscious of not having once enquired about the pony's health since the arrival of Moira.

"You couldn't be so cruel as to ride the poor little thing just after it had got a sprain, could you?" pursued Isabel.

"Not if it would hurt it, certainly; but, really, I can't keep Moira any longer. I will write to Papa to send me a very gentle horse."

"But do you know what those very gentle horses are capable of? I'll tell you. Didn't young Ben Rollston put his sister on one last summer, and didn't she come home all in little bits? And wasn't it a very gentle horse, a perfect lamb, that broke Kate Tynedale's collar-bone last May, and dragged her through a thickset hedge, and scratched her face all over? And didn't Harry Fitzover have his two front teeth kicked out by the horse his grandfather gave him, warranted gentle and free from tricks? I can assure you that you had better keep Moira, and if ever I want her I'll send down a groom for her. There'll be no use in returning her, for I'll send her back if you do. Your rides, or something, have done you ever so much good already. You look so much better,—doesn't she?" said Isabel, appealing to Walter.

Walter agreed that she did, and the conversation became general.

Isabel chatted quietly for awhile with Edith when they returned to the drawing-room, but soon she began to grow restless. She tangled the purple silk with which Edith was crocheting, she turned over the pages of the illustrated volumes on the table by which they were seated, she unsnapped and snapped her bracelets; in short, Isabel fidgeted.

" I wish Mrs. Arden wasn't talking to Mamma," she said, finally, looking at them regret-fully.

"Why?" asked Edith.

"Oh, then I would make her tell me stories; she knows ever so many horrid ones. I make her tell them whenever I spend the evening here. Did you never hear them?"

"No."

"What a pity," ejaculated Isabel, "I suppose we can't make her tell them now." She paused and reflected, then with sudden animation resumed, — "I know what we can do, we can make her give us the key of her private bookcase—she always keeps it locked, and we'll go upstairs and get some books and read the stories for ourselves, though it won't be half so good as if we, while she tells them, had her eyes to look at—I am sure she really believes them all."

Isabel approached Mrs. Arden with her request.

"Oh, yes, to be sure," replied that lady, ap-parently not sorry to have Isabel safely out of the room, for the clicking of the bracelets had been jarring her nerves. "There they are, my dear," and she produced from her pocket two small keys tied together. "Only please be sure to put back the books exactly in their places. Those you want are on the third and fourth shelves; and don't forget to bring me back the keys."

"Come," said Isabel in a low voice, returning to Edith's side, and holding up the keys. "We'll find something funny, you may be sure. I do so like to explore old ladies' crannies, don't you?"

"I never tried," said Edith, as they crossed the hall and ascended the staircase.

"It's great fun. I got Lady Chatterton to lend me her keys once, and you've no idea what things I found; and Mrs. Hammerthwaite—why her house is a perfect curiosity shop, for all it looks so precise and formal—I must tell you all about it some day, and how I got lost in it, and frightened one of the maids into hysterics. But here we are."

So saying, she applied the key to the bookcase in Mrs. Arden's sleeping-room.

"No; don't look at that, it's nothing," she continued, as Edith raised her hand to a crimson volume entitled " Sights and Sounds in the Cata-combs," "nothing worth reading; but just look over this ;" and she took down a small, well-worn book. "It's Norwyn's Diary. You wouldn't think it anything from the name, but when you've once begun it you can't stop. I got hold of it one day, and I begged Mrs. Arden to let me take it home with me, and I walked my horse and read all the way. The Bishop and some other people were coming to dinner, and I was not dressed in time, and I did not know what to say, for I only came down as they were going in. I thought the best thing was to tell the Bishop how it happened, and he said he didn't wonder at all, for that once when he was first in orders he began to read it before church, and it made him half an hour late for morning service."

Here Isabel, seeing Edith, who had begun to read, seat herself on the projecting ledge of the bookcase, with the volume in one hand and the candle in the other, began to explore the shelves in search of a book for herself. Apparently she found nothing to her taste, for she presently unlocked the door of the cupboard beneath and drew forth one volume after another. She was soon absorbed in the contents of a large book, bound in that purple and white marbled paper of which the French are so fond. She rose to her knees, holding it up to catch the light of the candle, and studied it intently for a while; then laying it down, a mischievous sparkle glittering in her eyes, remained plunged in thought. At length she replaced the books and locked the cupboard door.

"Come, don't you think we had better go down?" she said. "I think tea must be brought in by this time."

Edith mechanically descended from her post, still wrapt in the pages.

" Isn't it interesting?" asked Isabel. " But the first part is nothing to the middle and the end."

" Yes," replied Edith absently, following Isabel downstairs in silence. As soon .as they entered the drawing-room she sat down in a corner by a lamp, and went on with the narrative.

Isabel took her place near Mrs. Arden, behind a small japanned stand. She spread out her fingers upon it, and seemed to be at once studying her rings and listening to what Mrs. Arden was saying.

" I'm sure it's very kind in you to take any interest in the man, though he is in a pitiable state, very; but Walter is going to send him out of the country as soon as he can, to Canada with young Daubenay, and then no one will ever hear of him again, you know."

The stand behind which Isabel was sitting, here gave a slight lurch forward.

" Oh, the table—what's the matter with it?" exclaimed Isabel, but without removing her hands.

"What is it, my dear?" asked Mrs. Arden, turning her eyes towards Isabel.

"Oh! look, there it goes again," responded Isabel, as the table made a still more decided movement.

Mrs. Arden fell back in her chair. Lady Tremyss sat quietly observant.

"What is it?" repeated Isabel, as the table rocked backward and forward beneath her fingers.

Mrs. Arden raised her hand as if imploring silence whilst she collected her faculties of speech. At length, "There's a spirit in the room," she said, in a tremulous whisper.

The motion of the table immediately ceased.

"There, do you see that?" she continued, drawing still further into the recesses of her easy-chair. "It heard me."

"What are we to do?" inquired Isabel, anxiously. "It won't hurt us, will it?"

"I hope not; I'm sure I hope not," replied

G 5

Mrs. Arden, nervously; "but we must be very careful."

The table lurched forward.

"There it goes again!" ejaculated Isabel. "I'd rather not stay.  I think I'll go home."

"No! no!" exclaimed Mrs. Arden, affrightedly; "don't think of it;  don't take your hands away.  I don't know what would happen if you did.  Don't you see what it is?"

"No," answered Isabel.  "I don't see anything at all—I only feel the table jump."

The table nearly tipped itself over.

"It's the spirit getting impatient," responded Mrs. Arden in an awe-struck whisper.

"What does it want?" asked Isabel.

"It wants to tell something.  First, we must ask who it is.  That's the way they begin."

"Then you must ask," Isabel answered.  "I don't want to."

"Who are you?" inquired Mrs. Arden, in a trembling voice, staring at the chandelier.

There was no reply.

"Oh, I must say the letters—I quite forgot," said Mrs. Arden, hurriedly; and she began to repeat the alphabet. At Y the table moved.

"It's Y," she said tremulously, "Y."

A second trial gave the letter E.

"Y E, Ye. It's speaking to us all," said Mrs. Arden, apparently much relieved. But the succeeding letters decidedly impaired the consolatory effect of the first. Q U E N E came, much perplexing her mind.

"Isn't it old English?" asked Isabel. "Perhaps it means the Queen."

"Oh, gracious, you don't say so!" exclaimed Mrs. Arden, wildly. "What shall we do? Shall we go down on our knees?"

"I think we had better see if we can find out what queen it is," replied Isabel, in a somewhat unsteady tone, which Mrs. Arden took as an indication that even her nerves were not proof against the majestic presence of the unseen visitor.

E L I Z A B E T H came, letter by letter, to

increase Mrs. Arden's consternation.   But the
table left her no time for comment or reflection.
M E R C U R Y   A N D   S A T U R N
M E N A C E   C O N J U N C T I O N   L E T
T H O S E   W H O M   I T   C O N C E R N E T H
B E W A R E,   was the message delivered by
the supernatural visitant of the drawing-room.
Then the table resumed its pristine tranquillity,
and remained obstinately impervious to all Mrs.
Arden's entreaties that it would graciously deign
to explain its utterance.

" Well, I think no one now need attempt to
deny the existence of spirits," said Mrs. Arden,
after a pause.   " To think of it!—merely to
think of it!   And everything looks quite the
same as it did before," she continued, casting her
eyes around the room.   " It seems impossible before any one has seen it, and yet perfectly natural
after it has happened,—don't you think so ?" she
added, addressing Isabel.

" Yes, I do," Isabel responded; and, rising
abruptly, she seated herself near Edith, and,

turning her back to the rest of the room, seemed shaken by an internal agony. This Pythoness-like convulsion passed unnoticed by her hostess, whose mind had returned to the contemplation of the ominous warning conveyed by the table.

" ' Mercury and Saturn menace conjunction.' That means, according to Destrouyn's Manual, craft and power when they are alone; and when Mercury approaches Saturn, craft changes to treachery, and power becomes— what's the word? —maleficent, he says, and betokens the approach of an enemy. ' Let those whom it concerneth beware.' It must have meant some of us, or else it wouldn't have come here. Isabel was the near-est person. I hope it did not mean her," she said, turning to Lady Tremyss, who had sat an im-passive spectator.

" I do not fear anything for Isabel," replied Lady Tremyss, in her calm voice.

The tea-tray here appeared, interrupting Mrs. Arden's remarks ; and directly afterwards Walter came in.

No further mention was made of the spiritual experience which had taken place, unnoticed by Edith, who was still immersed in Norwyn's Diary, and unseen by Walter, who had been mentally comparing Edith and Isabel to the accompaniment of sips of sherry in the dining-room; for Mrs. Arden, great as was her desire to display this last conclusive proof, yet was withheld from so doing by the fear lest her recital should be received by Walter with an imprudent incredulity, which might bring back Queen Elizabeth, in all the grandeur of outraged and invisible dignity, to avenge herself by some one of those sudden outbreaks of rage, with which contemporaneous historians have made us familiar. —" If it had only been any spirit but Queen Elizabeth, I shouldn't feel so afraid," mentally soliloquised Mrs. Arden; " but she was a terrible woman, and there's no knowing what she might do if she got angry; perhaps she might hale us all about by the hair of our heads, as she did that poor lady who wanted to get married. I think I'd better not say anything about it, not even to Edith. Perhaps the next one will be Lady Jane Gray, and she wouldn't hurt anybody. Yes; I'll wait. But what could it have meant?"

When Lady Tremyss and Isabel had driven away, and Edith and Walter had retired to their respective apartments, Mrs. Arden unlocked the cupboard of her private bookcase, and drawing thence various volumes, studied their contents till one o'clock; though, judging from the expression of her countenance, she appeared in no wise enlightened when she ended.

A little note from Isabel, inviting Edith and Walter to take a drive with her mother and herself that afternoon, was brought to the Hall early the next morning; and punctual to the hour mentioned Isabel and Lady Tremyss appeared.

" Doesn't Mamma look like a beauty in that hat?" said Isabel to Edith. " She wears it on purpose to please me. I pulled all the feathers out as soon as it came down, and made Melvil put them in another way. Isn't it becoming?"

Becoming it certainly was, Edith thought, as Lady Tremyss stood in the hall, a wide black scarf draping her, the heavy plumes of her small black hat casting their shadow over her pale face.

"It looks like rain," said Isabel, descending the steps side by side with Edith. "Oh, if you want to see Mamma look her handsomest you should see her in a thunderstorm. Her eyes shoot out lightning, and—"

"Isabel," said Lady Tremyss' quiet tones from the carriage, "are you not keeping Miss Arden waiting?"

Isabel hurried forward.

"Tell him to take the Durston Road," she said to the footman, while Walter handed her into the carriage; "and tell him to drive fast."

" I'm sure we're going to have a shower," she repeated, taking her place opposite Edith.

" It's a pity," Edith replied.

"No it isn't, not a bit," responded Isabel, shaking her pretty head.

"Not in an open carriage?" queried Walter, with a glance at Edith's white muslin dress.

"Oh no, it won't hurt any of us, you'll see," rejoined Isabel.

Her eyes were dancing, she looked brimming over with suppressed merriment, and chattered like a mocking-bird as they drove forward, keeping the while an observant eye on all around. She detailed to them with infinitely comic fidelity of imitation, her experiment of the night before, and convulsed Walter and Edith with her rendering of Mrs. Arden's expression of countenance before the regal visitor from *outre vie*. At length a large white tent appeared in sight. Isabel pulled the check rein. The footman descended.

"Tell Jarvis to drive to that tent," she said peremptorily. The footman resumed his seat, and the carriage drove on.

"My dear," said Lady Tremyss, who had not

before spoken, "you cannot know what that tent is."

"Yes, I do," replied Isabel. "It's wild beasts, and I've brought you and Walter expressly to make it respectable, and I must go. I must, really and truly. I shall die if I don't. I dream about lions and tigers every night, because I haven't seen any, and now here they are, and they've come on purpose to be looked at."

"But nobody goes," Lady Tremyss objected.

"But we're not nobodies, we're somebodies; so what nobody does doesn't concern us," responded Isabel. "And what's the harm in going? Only because other people don't go. But I don't want to see other people there, I want to see the animals, and I've set my heart on it, and you'll let me, now won't you, you darling? You couldn't say no to me if you tried, you know you couldn't. May I go?" And Isabel looked smilingly in her mother's face.

A sharp contraction, as of pain, one instant furrowed Lady Tremyss' smooth forehead, then

leaning back she made a mute sign of assent.
Isabel clapped her hands.

" I knew you would. Ah, here we are! How
slow Gilbert is," she said, impatiently.

At that moment a low, deep growling was
heard from the tent. Edith drew back involuntarily. Glancing at Lady Tremyss, she saw a
sudden gleam escape from her eyes. She had no
time to watch her further, for just then the tardy
Gilbert threw open the carriage door.

" We had better take our cloaks with us," said
Lady Tremyss, standing up in the carriage,
and casting a glance at the black clouds that were
slowly rising from the west; " it may rain.—No
thank you, I will keep it," she added, as Walter
offered to relieve her of the heavy covering.
" You can carry Miss Arden's and Isabel's."

They entered the caravan.

" We will take our seats at once," said Lady
Tremyss. " The performances have begun. We
can walk round and let Isabel look at the animals
afterwards."

Leading the way to a vacant bench, she placed Edith by her side in the front row of the circle, while Isabel and Walter took their places directly behind.

As Edith gazed around, a very disagreeable sensation crept over her. She felt as though oppressed with nightmare. Her senses were assailed on every side by strange and bewildering sounds, sights, and odours. Above the heads of the circle of spectators she saw massive bars, behind which moved with restless, incessant motion, those monsters which had haunted her childish dreams. Their bright, fierce eyes glared at her; she beheld again the sharp white teeth which had so often in those terrified visions been ready to close upon her; the strong and penetrating odour acted peculiarly upon her nerves, producing in itself a sinking apprehensiveness. The low growlings, interspersed from time to time with angry snarls and plaintive, half-human cries, made a demoniacal concert.

Edith struggled against her nervousness; she

felt herself humiliated by her fears. Her will chafed against the thick coming fancies which assailed her imagination. She sought to turn aside her attention. She looked at the circling ranks of wondering and delighted rustic faces before her; she heard their shouts of laughter, while the keepers displayed the tricks of their trained dogs and ponies; she beheld the little deformed dwarfs, the monkeys, playing their grotesque antics, with almost human mockery, and closed her eyes in disgust, soon compelled by the fascination of fear again to open them again and turn them upon the ever-moving objects of her dread.

"Oh, look," said Isabel, in an excited whisper, "here comes the great elephant. I like him best of all."

As it advanced, the aspect of its sagacious, benevolent eye, the massive repose of its figure, scarcely disturbed by its slow, swaying tread, its friendly glance, when it received from the hands of the crowd its customary dainties, its look of patient, intelligent strength, communicated a moment's relief to Edith's fevered nerves. But her pleasure was of short duration. A faint flash of lightning glanced through the open roof, followed by a long, low, muttered roll of thunder. The animals moved more quickly up and down; they uttered discordant cries. The keepers looked around uneasily, then, glancing at the spectators, they whispered to each other. There was a pause in the performance. The crowd began to give signs of impatience. The sounds appeared to decide the keepers. They withdrew to the back of the caravan. " The great American panther, the only one ever tamed," Edith heard whispered around her, and every eye was turned to the open space in the circle.

Edith dared not ask any question. Surely they were not going to bring the animal there !

A murmur rose from the outskirts of the crowd of spectators; she looked, and saw a keeper enter, leading a panther by a leash. Its dark, sullen head held low, its sinister eyes glaring sideways on the audience, its tail swaying heavily, it was led along with slow, reluctant motion, to the centre of the ring. Suppressed exclamations of surprise and delight broke from the spectators as the animal, in unwilling obedience to the orders of the keeper, leaped through his arms, laid its paws on his shoulders, rolled over like a cat, and went through the round of its performances; but at every fresh command there was a pause before it obeyed, and those nearest could see that the keeper's eye watched observantly its every motion, while the elephant held itself aloof, eyeing it with an oblique, distrustful glance.

At length the exhibition of its accomplishments was over, and the keeper proceeded to lead it around the circle before it made its exit. He had taken but a few steps when a vivid flash of lightning, followed instantly by a loud crash of thunder, broke over the tent. The animal stopped short, cowered, and uttered a short cry. The keeper shook it by the leash and menaced it with his iron-handled whip. It snarled and proceeded. Its tail moved rapidly, lashing its flanks; its eyes glowed like burning emeralds. Edith's eyes followed its every step. Her fixed gaze seemed to draw towards her the creature's attention. As it reached the opposite side of the circle, it turned its head, and glanced around. Its look rested upon her white, shrinking figure. Again it stopped, it stretched out its neck, and gazed immoveably upon her. Again the keeper shook the leash, then with an affrighted shout, smote it with the iron handle. It crouched, rose in the air, and sprang full towards Edith.

A heavy mantle met the animal in its bound, enveloping the upper part of its body, blinding it; Lady Tremyss cast herself on the ground beside it, in the desperate endeavour to retain the folds about its head, whilst the panther, rolling over on its back, tore furiously at the mantle with its claws.

There was a moment of unutterable confusion, shrieks, cries, oaths, crashes, a trumpet-like roar, a ponderous rush, a piercing yell, and the panther lay writhing on two long white tusks, pinned to the ground by the elephant, which, with upcurled trunk, and tail erect, stood motionless, watching, with keen, expanded eye, the dying struggles of its foe.

One universal uproar rose from the cages around. The bars rattled as the excited animals within strove to break free. The terrified crowd pressed tumultuously towards the exit.

"This way, Madam, this way. You'll get soonest to the air this way."

The keepers opened a small door which led to a vacant enclosure without the tent. Walter carried out Edith, insensible. Two or three women attached to the caravan, came hurrying to her aid. As they bent over her with restoratives caught up in haste, Walter raised his eyes from her death-like countenance. He remembered the terrible face that had flashed before him with blazing eyes, and lips drawn back. He looked at Lady Tremyss. She was pacing up and down with rapid steps, her chest heaving, her nostrils dilated, impatient fire in her look.

Leaving Edith, Isabel sprang towards her.

"Mamma, Mamma, you are hurt; that's blood."

Snatching away the broad scarf that Lady Tremyss held closely about her, she showed her side, torn by the panther's claws.

" Don't stop me, let me breathe," said Lady Tremyss, throwing back the upper part of her figure with a gesture of wild strength. And she continued to pace up and down, like the creatures within.

" She's come to," exclaimed one of the women, joyfully. " Thank Heaven ! pretty dear."

"Lady Tremyss," said Edith, half inarticulately, as her senses returned. " I want Lady Tremyss."

Isabel dragged her mother towards her.

Edith rose staggering to her feet, and extending her arms, sought to throw herself on Lady Tremyss' neck. Lady Tremyss seized her wrists, and held her back.

" You have saved a life," said young Arden, hoarsely.

She answered nothing, but turned away.

Repulsing every offer of assistance, she entered the carriage. The horses sprang rapidly forward to escape the impending storm. Lady Tremyss did not speak, till in her usual quiet tone she bade Edith good afternoon, as Walter lifted her out at the Hall, with courteous hopes that her alarm might have no bad consequences.

# CHAPTER V.

THREE weeks had passed, during the course of which Mr. John Arden, Sir Joseph Slingsby, M.D., and Brenton, had made their appearance and disappearance at the Hall, and still Edith was confined to her room.

The palpitations which had followed her frigh t had been long and severe, leaving her in a state of great prostration.  Her father, summoned in haste, had arrived the next day, bringing with him the great London physician and Edith's maid.

The latter Edith, in an exhausted whisper, positively refused to  see; and Brenton was accordingly despatched to Arden Court by the

return train. Sir Joseph, after assuring Mr. Arden
that the case presented no alarming symptoms,
sent off, in his turn, for the physician of the shire
town, Dr. Jacobs, into whose hands he committed Edith, declaring to her father that she
was under as good care as was to be found in
England. He then took his leave, crossing, on
his way back, three separate telegrams sent to
summon him to three devout and titled believers,
who would have considered it little short of self-
immolation to commit their bodies to any other
skill.

Mr. John Arden made a longer stay, remaining
for the period of ten days, at the end of which
Dr. Jacobs politely dismissed him.

Like most men, Mr. John Arden was endowed
with an opaque want of comprehension as to
what was desirable in a sick room. He would
sit by his daughter's bedside, turning over the
morning papers in search of something to interest
her, when every rattling of the sheets was like
a blow upon her temples. He closed the

door whenever he came in or went out of her
chamber, with the extremest caution until it was
in its place; then suddenly relaxing his hold,
sent off the lock like a pistol.    He woke her up
with enquiries whether she were not hungry, and
kept her awake with regrets that he had disturbed
her; in short, with the best intentions in the
world, Mr. John Arden acted as if instigated by
the worst, and the result of his assiduous
attendance told so palpably upon his daughter's
state, that her physician, as we have said, was at
length forced to advise his return to Arden
Court.

His absence did not produce all the good
results that Dr. Jacobs had anticipated.    Edith's
restlessness diminished, it is true, but her depression increased.    Three weeks after he had been
first summoned, the physician sat at the foot of
her bed, surveying her with a puzzled aspect.

Dr. Jacobs was a man of about sixty,
with a broad forehead, and snow-white hair.
The lynx-eyed penetration that would have

been alarming in any other, in him was tempered
with such gentleness, such kindliness and charity,
that it lost all that was formidable, and served
but to give confidence in his ability.

As Dr. Jacobs sat with his eyes fixed upon
Edith's face, watching the weary gaze she had
fastened on the opposite wall, he heard a low
sigh break from her—a peculiar quivering sigh.

A sudden gleam of comprehension shot across
his face. He turned to Mrs. Arden and said,
" How old is she ?"

"Nearly seventeen," and Edith's aunt sighed as
though a world of woe were comprised in the
communication.

" Indeed! I had thought her much younger."

Dr. Jacobs studied Edith's face again. While he
looked, the hall door was unclosed, and the sound
of young Arden's voice came through the open
window.

A faint flush rose on the wan cheek.

Dr. Jacobs pressed his lips together and looked
down on the carpet, then rose and walked about

the chamber a little while.  Stopping before
Mrs. Arden, who by dint of anxiety had grown
to look as grim as a Gothic Saint, he said, cheerfully, "I think, Madam, that we must change
our treatment a little."

Mrs. Arden looked up eagerly.  Could it be !
Was Dr. Jacobs really going to try the
Panacea ?

Vain hope ;—his next words destroyed it.

" Yes.    We have tried entire rest and seclu-
sion long enough.  Now, if Miss Arden ap-
proves, we will have a little more variety and
amusement.    I think she needs toning.    We
must have some open air, and a little conversation."

Edith had turned her head, and was watching
him  intently.—Was she really going to see
Walter again ?  and how soon ?—She listened
eagerly.

" We will begin cautiously.  I think, perhaps,
it would be better that she should be dressed,
and taken into the next room.  She might see,

for instance, Mr. Arden for a few moments to-day, Miss Hartley a day or two later. But Miss Hartley is more of a stranger. We had better keep principally to the persons she is most accustomed to, for the present."

He approached the bed.

" Do you think you could try it, my dear ?"

After the first fortnight, he had always addressed Edith as " my dear."

She looked up and smiled. There was something in the smile that went to Dr. Jacobs' heart.

" I hope nothing will cross her," he said to himself as he went down stairs. " It might be one of those cases."

By one of " those cases," Dr. Jacobs was in the habit of mentally designating what is termed in the vulgate, "a broken heart." He always spoke of such instances as " cases of consumption."

During every waking moment of those long three weeks, Edith had longed for Walter's presence.

She craved the repose of contact with his strength, his cheerfulness, the exhilaration of his gaiety. His companionship had grown to be more than a luxury—it had become a necessity. Of all this Edith was aware, yet she had never gathered up together her various wants and needs and desires, and looked upon them and called them by their name. For a moment she had been bewildered by their newness, then she had decided that they were gratitude. It was gratitude that she felt. She was grateful to him, oh, so grateful!

And now it was gratitude that brought the light to her eye, the colour to her cheek, as when she was established on the couch in the next room, Walter was admitted and came to her side and took her outstretched hand. He was there. She had all she wanted.

"How merry they do sound," said Nitson to herself, raising her eyes from her work, while Walter's gay voice and Edith's low laugh came through the open door. "I should have thought if a young gentleman hadn't seen a young lady since she had been all but eaten up by a wild beast before his very eyes, that he'd feel, and she too, a little more solemn. But it isn't every one that has the same feelings."

And Nitson, a tall, pale, blue eyed woman, sighed.

Wanting in sentiment, although, according to Nitson's opinion, the interview had been, it nevertheless seemed to do her young mistress infinite good. Dr. Jacobs' nodded approvingly at her the next morning, and told her he saw that she meant to dismiss him as soon as possible. He moreover informed her that he had the day before received a note from Miss Hartley, imploring to be allowed to see her, and that he had consented that she should come for half an hour.

When he took his leave, Mrs. Arden followed him out, looking much disturbed. She fidgeted a little as a prelude, then ventured an inquiry.

" Of course you know best, I'm quite sure you do, of course—but Miss Hartley is so lively, you know—she is never still. If I were ill I would

as lief have six kittens in the room all at once, I
had really."

" Miss Hartley has more sense and feeling than
she shows," responded Dr. Jacobs. " You will
see, unless I am much mistaken."

Mrs. Arden, not daring to press the point
further, returned to Edith's room, there to await
the threatened visit.

" How kind in Isabel to have come every day !
I am glad that I am to see her.    And you are sure
that Lady Tremyss is quite well ?"

" Oh, yes, my dear, quite well, quite well,"
Mrs. Arden hurriedly replied, and knitted with
redoubled assiduity.   She did not like any reference to that day.   It frightened her, and she
was sure that it must frighten Edith also.   The
poor little woman was utterly incapable of com-
prehending the heroism with which her niece had
faced down the horror of the recollection.   Edith
was weak only with regard to what might be.
What had been, or what was, she could meet
unshrinkingly.

" I hear carriage wheels," said Edith, suddenly breaking the silence which had followed Mrs. Arden's reply. She half raised herself on the couch.

" Lie still, now do, please, my dear," implored Mrs. Arden, rising and going to the window. " Yes, it is Isabel, and—"

" And Lady Tremyss?" exclaimed Edith, her face flushing.

" Yes, but of course Lady Tremyss is not coming in. There, the carriage is turning."

While she spoke, quick steps were heard running along the gallery, and Isabel entered, bearing a basket of flowers. As she caught sight of Edith, she suddenly deposited her burden on the floor, and springing forward, knelt beside her, and laid her cheek on hers; then raising her head for a moment, she looked earnestly in Edith's face, her brown eyes glistening, and sat quietly down on the floor beside her, holding her hand.

Mrs. Arden glanced at her an instant over her

spectacles : Isabel was behaving better than she had expected.

As Isabel sat thus clasping her hand, a slow revolution began to work itself in Edith's thoughts concerning her. She became dimly conscious of depths in Isabel's nature at which she had not guessed, she vaguely felt that under her thoughtless vivacity, her childish recklessness, there lay a fund of undeveloped earnestness, a hidden reservoir of passionate strength. She turned and gazed in Isabel's eyes, then passing her arm around her neck, drew her towards her and kissed her.

" My dear, haven't you forgotten your flowers?" said Mrs. Arden after a pause, during which she had directed several perplexed glances at the two silent figures before her.—Mrs. Arden did not comprehend mute speech.

Isabel rose and brought the basket to Edith.

"How beautiful." she exclaimed, as her eye rested on the brilliant, strongly contrasted hues, "and the basket, how pretty it is."

" Do you like it ? I am very glad ! Mamma set me working it for you when I was so miserable because I came away every day without seeing you. She drew the pattern, and showed me how."

" Did she invent the flowers ?" aksed Edith, examining the graceful outline and gorgeous colouring of the wreath of embroidery that encircled the basket. " They look as if they must be real; and yet I never saw any such."

" I asked her if she had made them up, and she said no," answered Isabel. " She always draws her own patterns. She never copies any of the flowers in the garden or the conservatory; but I once found some like them engraved in a book of Mrs. Lacy's."

" Is she really quite well now ?" asked Edith, unconsciously paling a little.

" Yes," said Isabel; then lowering her tone, she added, " When you see her, don't say anything. She won't like it."

" No," replied Edith, sinking her voice likewise. " But why ?"

"I don't know. All the county has called just as they have here; and sent messages, and all that; but mamma wouldn't receive, and always sent word that she was perfectly well. But she could not wear a tight dress for more than a fortnight; beg all I could, she wouldn't have the doctor, and she wouldn't let me see the place."

"I won't say anything," whispered Edith, as Isabel, glancing at her watch, rose to leave her; "but tell her how I feel."

She took Isabel's two hands and looked earnestly at her.

"Yes," replied Isabel, "I'll tell her. When would you like to see her? She'll come."

It was arranged that Lady Tremyss should call the next day.

Punctual to Isabel's appointment Lady Tremyss came. Her visit was at once a relief and a disappointment to Edith. The scene at the caravan had to all appearance passed totally from her preserver's mind.

# CHAPTER VI.

"WELL, Doctor, how do you find your patient this morning," said Walter, as he met Dr. Jacobs in the hall a day or two later,

"We are doing very well. We are promoted to beefsteak and old port to-day."

"Old port," repeated young Arden, rather dubiously. "Are you not afraid it may act on her nerves?"

"I hope it will. That's what I give it for. But why do you wish that it should not?"

"Oh, I know nothing about it," replied the young man,—"only if it were to make her see disagreeable things."

Dr. Jacobs laughed.

" A wine-glassfull would scarcely do that."

" But a wine-glassfull did do that," replied Walter gravely.

Dr. Jacobs stopped laughing. His professional curiosity was roused.—Had young Arden really discovered any person so peculiarly open to the action of stimulants? It was worth while finding out what he meant.

" Just explain, won't you. Do you mean to say that you ever met any one over three years of age, who could be seriously affected by a glass of wine?"

" Certainly. It struck me as strange, but it happened only a few weeks ago. That groom of Sir Ralph's, who was so much abused at the time of the accident,—you remember?"

" Yes."

" Well, he came here and was taken ill. Frintly ordered him a sedative, and Witchkin's assistant sent him port wine by mistake. It produced the strangest effect upon him,—made him see visions."

Dr. Jacobs raised his eye-brows incredulously.

"What sort of visions?"

"According to his account, painfully distinct —a procession of disagreeable faces."

"It wasn't port wine. It was an opiate—an overdose."

"But Witchkin's assistant confessed to having made the mistake, and having sent port wine instead of the prescription."

"Then he lied."

"But it wasn't the first time it had happened. He took a glass the day Sir Ralph was drowned, and it produced the same effect."

Dr. Jacobs shot a quick glance at his companion.

"Indeed ! Who gave it to him?"

"The butler at the Park, Goliath."

Dr. Jacobs' eyebrows lowered over his eyes. He compressed his lips, and stood a moment in thought, then looking up, said,

"Where was this groom when he took the supposed sedative?"

" At Mrs. Dingall's; one of the people on the Tremyss estate."

" Can you give me the direction ?"

Walter gave the address.

"It is a very curious case. I think I shall call and find out all I can about it. One can't get too much light on such matters, you know."

Dr. Jacobs drove away in the direction of Mrs. Dingall's.

Mrs. Dingall had been busy at the wash-tub, when the unaccustomed event of a vehicle stopping at her door, brought her out.

" Is your name Dingall, my good woman ?"

" Yes, Sir, if you please, Sir," answered Mrs. Dingall, looking alarmed. All her surprises in life, poor woman, had been of a disagreeable nature; accordingly she looked distrustfully at this new one, personified in Dr. Jacobs.

" There was a man, a groom, staying here, ill, awhile ago, I believe.'

" Yes, Sir, but he's gone, Sir ; he went a week

ago to-day. Mr. Arden sent him off to Canada, Sir."

She looked up as if that were well off her mind. Surely now the visitor would go away.

But no. Dr. Jacobs gave no sign of moving.

" When he was ill, there was a mistake about some medicine, I believe."

" Yes, Sir ; but it wasn't I, Sir. It was the apothecary's young man, Sir."

" Yes, I know you were not at all to blame."

" Thank you, Sir," said Mrs. Dingall, courtseying and looking somewhat relieved.

" Who was it that took the prescription to be made up?"

Mrs. Dingall's fears returned in full force.

" It was I, Sir, but I brought it home just as it was given to me. Nobody ever thought of blaming me, Sir."

"Of course not. Then you saw it made up ?"

" Yes, Sir. I saw the young man take the big bottle down, and measure it and pour it into a little one."

This improbable statement appeared in no

wise to diminish the interest with which Dr. Jacobs was listening to her communication.

"And then what did he do?"

"Then he poured in a little of something yellow, Sir,"            .

"Syrup," said Dr. Jacobs to himself.

"And then—?"

"And then, yes, Sir, then he filled it up with something that looked like water."

"Very well, you observed very well. Now can you tell me where the large bottle stood, out of which he poured the first liquid into the little bottle that he gave you?"

"Yes, Sir," responded Mrs. Dingall promptly, inspired by the comfortable belief that since the gentleman had praised her, no harm was coming of it. "He turned round and took it from the shelf just behind him."

"Where was he standing?"

"Behind the scales, Sir. I noticed it because he rested his chin on the top of them when he asked me what I wanted."

"Which shelf did he take it from?"

" I don't know, Sir. It wasn't from the top ones."

Dr. Jacobs paused and cogitated. Mrs. Dingall, her fears allayed, began to remember regretfully the warm soap suds. They would certainly get cold. She shifted her weight from one foot to the other, with a sort of meek impatience.

" Was it not rather queer, his resting his chin on the top of the balance ?"

" Yes, Sir,—the young man was rather queer, Sir ?"

" How ?"

" Why, he seemed a sort of 'mazed like, Sir. He was uncommon polite, and called me 'Sir,' all the time."

Dr. Jacobs meditated anew. Mrs. Dingall stole sideways to the door of the cottage and looked in. The tub was still steaming. She took courage and returned.

" Was there any label on the bottle ? "

" No, Sir."

" Unpardonable carelessness, that," commented Dr. Jacobs.

" Then he gave you the bottle, and you took it directly home ? "

" Yes, Sir. I never let it go out of my hand till I gave it to him here, Sir."

" Pray have you any of the bottles used when the groom was ill ? "

" Oh, yes, Sir, I've got them all. You don't think I'd throw anything away, Sir ! "—in a tone of deprecatory surprise.

"Oh, very well," said Dr. Jacobs, brightening up. " Sometimes it's the best thing people can do to throw physic away, but it wouldn't have been so here. Would you be so good as to bring me those bottles ? and then I won't detain you any longer."

Mrs. Dingall withdrew, her motions quickened by the unmistakeable vision of the strange gentleman's hand approaching the strange gentleman's pocket.

She was gone longer than Dr. Jacobs had expected. Finally she reappeared, holding two brightly shining glass phials.

" Eh--Oh,--What's that ! " exclaimed Dr. Jacobs.

" I'm sorry to have kept you waiting, Sir, but they were dirty and I washed them out, Sir. Now they look as clean as need be."

And she held them up triumphantly.

" The corks, you didn't wash the corks, did you ?" said Dr. Jacobs, catching at a ray of hope.

" No, Sir, I'm very sorry, Sir," responded Mrs. Dingall, penitently, perceiving that something was wrong, " but, I beg pardon, Sir, they smelt bad, Sir, and I didn't think they would be useful, and so I just dropped them into the fire, Sir."

Dr. Jacobs silently put a shilling into Mrs. Dingall's hand, and turned his horse away.

There was something here to be found out. He had been foiled at the woman's with regard to the bottles, but he had, nevertheless, got some important information. He was very nearly sure it was not port wine that Mrs. Dingall had carried home. Now to Witchkin's, to verify the position of the large bottle, and find out the truth of the story as to the alleged mistake.

Mr. Barrows presented himself to Dr. Jacobs' eyes as he entered the shop. He stood for an instant, studying the assistant's appearance.

" Unsatisfactory," thought Dr. Jacobs to himself. He advanced to that part of the counter where the scales were suspended, and cast a glance along the rows of bottles. There it was, just where Mrs. Dingall had seen it. Then why on earth had the assistant said he had made a mistake ?

Dr. Jacobs looked again at him. Mr. Barrows meekly advanced. He did not exactly like the investigating expression of the stranger's face, for Mr. Barrows had but recently made his appearance in the shop, and Dr. Jacobs was a stranger to him.

" A fine morning, Sir," he said, with a lacklustre glance at that portion of the sky visible between the coloured jars in the window.

" A very fine morning, enough to make all the sick people well."

" Well, Sir, I hope not."

And Mr. Barrows gave a melancholy smile, that would have suited a sentimental vampire.

" Oh, you think that would not suit you."

" No, Sir, there's not much doing any way. The country is a dreadfully healthy place, Sir."

And he looked more depressed than before.

" Yet the country people have their ailments. One of the finest young fellows I ever saw, was pulled down a week or two ago at Mrs. Dingall's "

" Very like, Sir; but I don't know the name."

" Perhaps you would know her. She was a pale faced woman, with both of her front teeth gone. She brought a prescription for a sedative from Dr. Frintly ?"

" Don't know,—can't tell, Sir."

" Don't you remember ? There was some mistake about it. You sent port wine instead, didn't you ?"

Mr. Barrows' face took an expression of hopeless perplexity.

" I am sure I don't know, Sir."

" Have you got the prescription?"

" I can look, Sir."

Opening a large book, he began feebly to turn
over the pages.

" Give it here," said Dr. Jacobs; and in a few
moments he paused at Dr. Frintly's prescription.

" There, do you see that?"

" Yes, Sir."

" What did you give the woman that brought
it?"

" I gave her the prescription, Sir."

" Then why did you tell Dr. Frintly that you
gave her port wine?"

Barrows, feeling that his wits were leaving
him, groaned aloud.

" Come, answer me; why did you say that?"

" I suppose it must have been true, Sir."

" But don't you know? Can't you tell the
truth now?"

" If I knew, I would, Sir."

Whereupon Dr. Jacobs, giving up the interrogatory as useless, left the shop.

" The fellow is an idiot," he thought to himself, as he drove down the village street, greatly disturbing some stray geese, and loudly acclaimed by some round-cheeked children, who, running after him, with an instinctive perception that they were safe from any unsympathising cut from the whip, scrambled up behind,—" an idiot. What the woman said settles the question. The man took a sedative, an over-dose. He describes the usual symptoms, says he has experienced them before, gives as a date the evening of Sir Ralph's death, and names the butler as the person who gave it to him. But, perhaps, he had the tooth-ache, or some ache or other, and some of the women in the house—women are always playing doctor—had given him an anodyne, and he had ascribed its effects to the port wine. That's much more probable. And the man is not here to question. I fancy I have given myself a good deal of trouble about nothing."

So saying, Dr. Jacobs dismissed the subject from his mind.

And Nemesis drew back into her shadowy hand the clue that had fallen from the good doctor's careless hold, and waited and watched again.

# CHAPTER VII.

As Dr. Jacobs had predicted, Edith soon dismissed him, or rather he declared that he had more serious matters on hand than coming every day to assure himself that she did not need his services. Accordingly he withdrew, and Edith was left to the sole care of Mrs. Arden, who, sharing the disinclination to out-door exercise that marks most ladies of her age, laid that portion of the charge which necessitated drives, rides, and when Edith grew stronger, walks, upon Walter.

One afternoon they had strolled together in the direction of the village church. They had taken a woodland path, and had loitered along. The close of the summer had passed while Edith was

shut up, and now the autumn was come.   The
soft hues, the tender sadness,  the regretful quiet
of  the  season,  harmonized  with  the  naturally
subdued  tone  of  Edith's  spirits.   The dreamy
stillness  of  the autumn  woods,  scarce  disturbed
by the momentary  appearance of  a little brown
rabbit  or  leaping  hare,  seemed  a  spell  around
them both.   They  scarcely spoke, wandering on
in silence as if they feared  to disturb  some unreal habitant.    At length they came to the border
of  the  woodland :  the  little  church  lay  before
them, grey, peaceful, solemn.

Drawn  by  that  sense  and  love  of  contrast
which we so often see in  the young, they entered
the churchyard  and wandered  amid  the  graves,
stooping here and there  to  decipher some  moss-
grown inscription, or to part the weeds from some
tiny head-stone which told that an infant lay beneath.

Edith seated herself upon  the  low  wall,  and
gazed around.  The sun was sinking in the western
sky,  a  few  amber  clouds  floated  high  over  head,

the chirping of birds came from the old trees that surrounded the quiet spot.

" How much better to lie here than under the stone pavement of the church," she said. " How sad for those who have loved them to stand Sunday after Sunday above the vaults, and think of those who lie there cold and still, deaf to the chanting, dumb in the responses—so near, yet gone for ever."

" And yet it almost seems that the dead may like to be grieved for," answered Walter, whose associations were perhaps more classic than Christian.

" If they truly loved they would wish the living to be happy," said Edith. " How dreadful it must be for Lady Tremyss to think of her husband, who was so fond of her, buried under her very feet."

" But he is not," replied Walter.

" Why? I thought the Tremyss tomb was there. Are not the Tremyss monuments in the church ?"

" Certainly ; but Sir Ralph is not there."

" Why not ?"

" His body was not found.   The river is deep,
and full of rocks and holes.   They dragged it for
miles, but the body had got caught somewhere.
It never rose."

" And perhaps it is still there, close to his
home ?"

" No one can say."

" It may be that the sphynxes know and cannot tell.   Do you not remember that first day?"

" Yes, I remember.   You said they looked as
if they knew something."

" How can she bear to live there with that
cruel, treacherous river running past her very
gate?"

" Use, you know ; besides, the park is her property.   It was left to her.   She would not like to
give it up."

" Did Sir Ralph leave her all his property ?"

" Everything he could dispose of he settled
upon her."

"I thought estates usually went to men?"

"There was no entail on the property he inherited from his mother. He could do with it as he liked. But the sun is going down; had we not better return?"

"You will think me more foolish than ever," replied Edith, rising reluctantly; "but I really don't like the idea of crossing that river."

"I never think you foolish, you know; and it is quite comprehensible why this evening the river should be disagreeable. We had better go home by the road, it is the shortest way."

Leaving the churchyard they walked in the direction of the river, which lay between them and Arden Hall.

They reached at length the bridge, a single Roman arch, whose solid masonry still firmly spanned the rushing water below. Edith stopped and looked over the stone parapet.

"Where was it that he fell in?" she asked, looking up the river. "Ilton Park is higher than this, it must have been at some distance."

" I was away, and do not know exactly ; but anyone in the neighbourhood could tell."

" I want to know, because then there will be only one place to feel uncomfortable at passing ; otherwise the whole river is dreadful."

She drew back.

Walter saw that Edith was distressed. She must be satisfied immediately. He looked around. A group of children were playing at marbles near by.

" Here, boy," he called.

They raised their shock heads, looked distrustfully at him an instant, as if he were a beadle in disguise, then whispered hurriedly together. The result of their conference was the pushing forward of a staring-eyed boy, who advanced a few steps, and then stood immoveable, mindless of the admonitions of the rest.

" Do you live in this neighbourhood ?"

" 'Tisn't me he wants, it's Jem," responded the offered-up boy, looking over his shoulder, then facing round and beating a sudden retreat.

" Go 'long with you, Jem, doan't ye keep the
gentleman waiting," vociferated the shock-headed
chorus, the secret of whose reluctance to approach lay in the vivid recollection of a foray
executed upon the Arden orchard a few evenings
previously, and a perfect knowledge of the personal identity of the handsome young gentleman
before them.

Thus adjured, Jem, a small, sharp-visaged
youth of about ten, reluctantly advanced.

" Do you live near by ?"

" E'es, Sir ; I lives down there," pointing to a miserable little cottage close to
the water's edge. He then glanced ruefully
round at his companions. They were stealing
away. If Jem had been found out and had got
to be trounced, so much the worse for him.
Staying and seeing it wouldn't help him. Jem,
seeing himself deserted, looked beseechingly in
Walter's face.

" I'll give you a shilling if you can tell me
where Sir Ralph fell in."

He drew the coin from his pocket.

Every muscle of Jem's face reversed its position; his sharp eyes shone, he stretched out his hand; then a slow eclipse spread over his face, and he dropped his arm with a perplexed and doleful look.

" What, don't you know?"

" I know's summ'at, Sir."

" Then tell all you know, and you shall have it."

The boy gazed longingly at the shilling.

" Can't you speak?   Well, if you don't want it—"

And young Arden was about to put it back in his pocket.   The boy jumped like a fish on a line.

" Please, Sir, let me think a bit, Sir."

" Be quick, then.   Why are you so long about it?" said Walter, beginning to lose patience.

" You won't never tell nobody, Sir, what I says to you if I'll tell?"

" No.   I only want this young lady to know."

" Well, Sir," said the lad in a confidential whisper, coming nearer, " Daddy had some lines out here and some more down the river that night, and he set me a watching of these. And as I was watching down there," he pointed to a spot near the bridge, " I heerd a horse galloping along the road, and I scuttled away and hid myself under the bridge; but I peeped, and I spied Sir Ralph. He was going like mad. The moon was out. I knew him well enough : it wasn't a week since he'd laid his whip over my shoulders for being in the road as he drove by. When he'd got past I came out again, and in a little while I heerd a sort of a roar, like, come down the river. I was scared at it, Sir, it was such a sound, and I thought to myself—there's the devil has got Sir Ralph at last,—and I crept under the bridge again. And the next morning I heerd as how Sir Ralph was drownded. They said it was swimming of the river in front of the park, but it wasn't true, Sir. I seen him, Sir, as plain as I sees you; but Daddy would have thrashed me if I had let on a word to any body, 'cause as how then it would have come out about the lines."

"Strange, " said young Arden thoughtfully. " Did you never tell your father?"

" No, sir. Daddy was in a thundering fury that night 'cause as how he'd had bad luck; and he basted me 'cause the fish hadn't risen. So I kept clean out of his way at first, and afterwards I didn't think to tell."

Walter tossed the boy the shilling, and turned to Edith.

" Well, you have heard. You won't be afraid to cross the bridge now? I thought it was directly in front of the Park, but I wasn't sure. I wonder the boy should have heard so distinctly. However, sound travels far on water, especially at night."

"That must have been the same shout the servants heard."

And Edith repeated Mrs. Dingall's ghost story.

" That isn't likely. No one could have heard

such a distance through the close timber of the Park."

" But they said it woke them up."

" Don't you see that must have been impossible? The house stands more than half a mile from the road."

" It must have been something."

" Probably an owl,—owls are the fathers of half the ghost stories going ;—or it may have been that one servant screamed in a dream and woke the rest up, and as it happened to be on the night Sir Ralph was drowned, of course they declared it was his ghost come to inform them. The superstition of those people is exasperating."

They walked on in silence for some time, then Walter suddenly exclaimed

" I don't understand it at all."

" What?" asked Edith, " the ghost?"

" That lad's story. How did the horse get into the river?"

" It might have run away and swam across."

" It wouldn't have been likely to swim away

from home. And besides, I remember hearing that it was found on the Park side of the river."

" What do you think, then ?" asked Edith, uneasily.

" I don't know what to think. There's some catch in the story. I wish I had been here at the time."

The subject dropped, and they walked silently on.

As they turned from the road into a narrow lane that led to the Hall they heard the sound of hoofs. They looked back. Lady Tremyss, in her black habit, and Isabel, in her riding-dress of pale grey, shot past like phantoms.

Edith and Walter watched them until the misty shadows hid their fast receding figures. They seemed to Edith to have vanished into another world.

# CHAPTER VIII.

Since the time of Edith's illness, Isabel had been an almost daily visitor at the Hall. One of those friendships which sometimes so strangely link to each other opposite natures, had sprung up between the two girls, so dissimilar in appearance, in education, in taste, and in character.

On Isabel's side the attachment was the more enthusiastic, certainly, yet she appeared satisfied with the quiet affection which Edith tendered her. Its very tranquillity seemed to be to her one charm the more.

Her habit was to gallop over from the Park after breakfast, to spend the morning with Edith, and to gallop back to lunch. She seemed to have no definite aim in these visits, except to be in Edith's presence. Often she would lie on the floor the whole morning, her head resting on her arms, her face perfectly motionless, her eyes watching Edith's every motion; then, when mid-day approached, she would rise from her recumbent position, kiss Edith on her forehead, or her cheek, or her neck, or her hand—she never kissed her on the lips—and go away, having spoken scarcely a word.

Edith had at first attempted to induce her visitor to lie on the sofa; but Isabel's look of discomfort pleaded so powerfully against the enforced luxury, that her hostess was fain, after a few reluctant efforts on Isabel's part, to allow her to return to her favourite resting-place on the floor.

Little by little she grew accustomed to Isabel's private ways, which were as unlike as possible to those which she displayed in public. Edith would read, draw, work, and think with perfect disregard to Isabel's presence, from time to time looking up and gazing an instant on the beautiful face that lay watching her with such strange fixedness. Then the shadow of a smile would rise in Isabel's brown eyes, as if she heard the distant song of a bird, or caught a gleam of sunlight on falling water. Sometimes she would rise from her recumbent position, and drawing up her knees and resting her chin on them, would sit plunged in reverie. If Edith asked what she was thinking of, she would answer.— " Nothing."

But these fits of silence and reverie would pass off, and leave Isabel the same gay, laughing, playful being as before. Then she would chatter by the hour together, apparently not much caring whether Edith listened or not.

She would mimic all her acquaintance, from the rector, a pompous personage, who officiated but rarely, down to Dame Barlow, a red-eyed old woman, afflicted with a lamentable stammer. She could mock the sound of every feathered or four-footed creature, and would take an elfish delight in provoking them to trials of skill. In short, nothing could be more capricious, more desultory, or more perplexing, than her moods, her occupations, and her fancies; yet through all these ran a vein of originality which engaged Edith's interest.

It was about a fortnight after Edith's walk to the churchyard. The morning was sunny, the light poured brightly into the great sitting-room which had been appropriated to Edith's use since her arrival at the Hall. Edith sat at a table near the window, drawing. Isabel lay lounging in an easy chair, her dark riding habit showing every outline of her symmetrical figure. Her hat was cast on the floor beside her, in company with her riding-whip and gloves; her long, curling lashes almost touched her cheek as she lay, her eyes bent on the floor. At length she broke silence with a sigh. The sound was new to Edith. She had never heard Isabel sigh before. All her fits of silence had seemed pure introversion—no sadness had mingled with them. She raised her head.

" What is it, Isabel ? "

" It's something dreadful," was Isabel's reply.

Edith dropped her pencil and came towards her. She seated herself on the elbow of the easy chair.

" What is it? Won't you tell me ? "

" I've always been so happy, and now I'm almost seventeen,—in a month it will be my birthday."

The discord which Isabel apparently perceived between her past happiness and the vicinity of seventeen, was not equally visible to Edith's perceptions.

" Well," she said, as if expecting a more distinct explanation of the sigh.

" But it isn't well. I feel,—I don't know how I feel,—as if I were going to be a stranger, —as if all were to be changed, and as if I should lose myself in it."

She turned a half appealing look to Edith.

" Tell me all about it.  Try to think it out,"
said Edith softly.

" I  can't," said  Isabel, shaking  her  head.
" Besides, I  don't want to.  What would you
say if  I told  you  that I felt as if I could be
wicked ?"

" I  shouldn't  be  afraid," replied Edith, " I
know you would not hurt me, and I don't believe
you would hurt any one else."

" Yes, but I might hurt  myself," said Isabel
gloomily.  Then, springing up hastily, she passed
her hand through the masses of her hair, tossing
them down with a quick impatient ges ture.

" I have a had bad dream I think.   I don't believe it was myself.'

She went to the window, looked out over the
even sweep of the lawn, gazed an instant at the
blue  sky,  tormented a canary  by executing an
impossible cadenza, wound up  her  hair again,
kissed Edith, and left the room.

" You ought to have  read  up for this evening,

ladies," said Walter, coming into the parlour where Edith had joined her aunt, some hours later. Here's a note from Mr. Tracey, to say that Mr. Hungerford, the great traveller, has just come down to stay with him, and asking leave to bring him. You won't shine, Edith, unless you are well up in Mexican architecture and North American earthworks."

"Dear me, you don't say so. What shall I do?" exclaimed his aunt, suddenly passing into a state of extreme and anxious perplexity. " I never talked to a great traveller in all my life. I shan't know in the least what to say to him. I wish he hadn't come down; I'm sure he'll find it stupid. And as to reading up, I wonder you should speak of such a thing, Walter, when you know I haven't got any time. Here it is three o'clock, and we dine at seven."

"But if you were to take the Encyclopedia, and read up Canada—that's where he was last," replied Walter gravely,—" I don't think it would take long."

" Don't mind him, Auntie, he's only teasing you," said Edith, consolingly.    " Mr. Hungerford will be very pleasant. We had Dr. Spracklin to dine, and he was such a nice, chatty little man.''

" Mind, Aunt Arden, that you put Edith near him.    Perhaps she would like to have him take her in to dinner," interposed Walter.

" Oh, but I can't, I can't indeed ;  the table is all arranged.    Dear me, Walter, here I was just quieting myself down for the evening, and you've upset me again.    My nerves are all in a quiver ; I wish you'd go away and not stand there looking so provoking.    Edith can't go in with Mr. Hungerford, that is, unless she wants to—but you don't, do you, my dear ?" she said imploringly, addressing her niece.

Thus adjured, Edith professed perfect willingness to go in with any one whom her aunt might choose.    But Walter, having ascertained Edith's private wishes, manœuvred until he had modified the dinner table arrangements so that Edith should have the traveller opposite her.

"Not that it will do you much good," he added, when communicating the result of his tactics to Edith. "He won't talk—nobody ever talks at these dinner parties. They're more stupid than you can imagine."

"I don't think it will be so bad," Edith returned. "Besides, I can always find amusement in watching new faces, even if the people don't open their lips."

"I'm glad you will have that resource: you'll need it," Walter responded. "Six times a year I'm bored to death, and on each occasion it happens to be at one of our own dinner parties. But I never say anything, for they're an institution. Aunt Arden would as soon give up Church and State."

When Walter entered the drawing-room that evening, Edith's back was turned towards him. At first he hardly recognized her in her trailing length of skirt, her curls shortened and raised, freeing the graceful outlines of her neck and shoulders and imparting an unaccustomed dignity to her appearance. As she turned at his approach he half drew back. A painful sensation, as if she had been suddenly snatched to a distance from him, ran through his mind, mingling with his admiration a sharp pang of regret. He had felt her so near, so dear, so childlike, so clinging; and now, by some inexplicable mystery, she stood before him, a graceful young woman, no longer the Edith of every day, but something older and more beautiful, perhaps inaccessible.

She looked up at him and smiled. The smile, the eyes, were the same.

"You don't say anything. Don't you like Edith's dress? I am sure you must," said Mrs. Arden. "She has turned quite into a young lady, you see."

"I see," responded Walter; then, with an effort, he continued. "But how magnificent you look yourself. It seems to me that there never was so much of you before."

He turned his eyes upon her ample sweep of velvet folds, and upon the rich *parure* of old point which completed er costume.

"It's all Edith's fault," replied Mrs. Arden, looking a little ashamed. "She made me order a new dress, and ransacked all my things till she came across this lace, and she told Nitson how to make it up; and she said I must wear it to please her, and so of course I did, you know."

"Wasn't I right, and isn't it becoming?" asked Edith, gazing affectionately at her aunt's diminutive figure and features, set off as they were by her well chosen toilette.

"Do tell me what you think about Edith?" repeated Mrs. Arden. "How do you think she looks to-night?"

Edith, who had been used since her earliest childhood to hear her appearance commented upon, turned an unembarrassed glance towards him. She did not care much about it herself, but she would be glad to have Walter like it.

"I liked to see her better as she was before," he answered; and, turning away, he employed himself in re-arranging some engravings which lay upon a table at a little distance.

Under a certain sort of provocation Edith was anything but patient. Her eyes sparkled and her colour rose at Walter's tone of cold and almost rude dissatisfaction.

" Dear me, how very odd Walter is to-night," said his aunt, in an aggrieved tone. " I never saw him so before. Don't care for it, dear,—you look perfectly lovely." And she left the room to ask a question that she had forgotten.

Edith sat down on a low couch and gazed silently into the fire.

Walter turned his head and looked at her. He knew that he had vexed her. He hastily approached.

" You never looked so well as you do to-night."

She raised her eyes. There was that in his tone that disarmed her anger at once.

" Then why— ?"

" Don't ask me," he replied, abruptly, and returned to the engravings.

—Why ?—he shrank from thinking.

Mrs. Arden returned and hurried up the room as a carriage drove up to the hall door.

"I am so sorry that almost all the people excepting Lady Tremyss will be strangers, quite strangers to you, my dear," she said, as if struck by a sudden thought. "I ought to have had Isabel, I really had. But then she never comes, and I never thought of it."

"I am used to strangers; I don't mind them," Edith answered, smiling.

—Walter was not displeased with her. There was nothing else that could disturb her now.— The guests arrived, closely following each other. At length Mr. Tracey and Mr. Hungerford were announced. Edith instantly singled out the *savant*, a small, thin, wiry man, with projecting eyebrows, mobile features, and bronzed complexion. As he was introduced to Edith after his reception by Mrs. Arden, his expression changed. He smiled, and, addressing some little compliment to her, entered into conversation.

—It is something quite wonderful, the link of

sympathy which draws together men of study and
science, and pretty young girls. What they
talk about together, what mutual ground they
find to meet upon, is an unsolvable mystery; but
the fact is there :—to the utter disgust and discom-
fiture of their younger and more eligible rivals, the
brightest glances and sweetest smiles are rained
upon men who at other moments clasp " ologies "
to their bosoms.

While Lady Tremyss entered the room, Mr.
Hungerford's eye rested attentively upon her.
He broke off what he was saying, with an
enquiry.

" Who is that? I did not hear the name."

" Lady Tremyss. Very beautiful, is she
not ?"

" Singularly so."

" And so graceful."

" Yes. It is a peculiar grace. She does not
walk like an Englishwoman."

" I have often thought that she did not look
English."

"Indeed! and yet I perceive what you mean. She is darker than one usually sees, but her features are purely English."

Here dinner was announced, and young Renson with his ten thousand a year, who had stood internally puffing and fuming at seeing the attention of the young lady who should have fallen to his share as by predestined right, thus engrossed, advanced to claim Edith, and snatch her from the *griffes* of the London lion.

Edith surveyed the dinner table when she found herself fairly seated. On her right was young Renson, a red faced youth, with uproarious whiskers, small grey eyes, ordinary forehead, and strictly correct costume. On her left sat Colonel Pycherly, a middle-aged man, with unmeaning blue eyes, a long nose, and a small mouth and chin, which seemed from their want of size to be quite unable to meet the steady demand he was in the habit of making upon their receptive powers. At the end of the table sat Walter and Lady Emily Marsh, the latter

composed of a scarlet velvet dress, a white lace
shawl, a towering head dress, and a set of
emeralds.     Edith looked at her several times
without being able to perceive anything but these
articles of attire.    Her eye slipped involuntarily
over Lady Emily's *effacé* features and vacant expression.    On Walter's right, turning the corner
of the table, sat Mrs. Tinedale, a brunette, with
fine eyes, and irregular features.    Next her, Mr
Hungerford ; beyond him, a solid embankment
of snow and pink silk, together forming Mrs.
Powell,   quite obstructing the view down the
table and presenting an impenetrable breastwork ;
with her *vis-à-vis*, Colonel Pycherly, isolating
Edith's end of the table.    She looked for Lady
Tremyss, but the great *épergne* with its drooping
flowers stood between.

"Walter was right," was the mental result of
her rapid reconnoissance. " How dreadfully stupid
it is going to be ! "

So thinking, Edith hopelessly resigned herself
to inevitable *ennui*.

The soup plates, as is their custom, appeared to impose a reverential awe upon the guests. The first course passed in silence, broken only by an observation from young Renson to Edith, conveyed in a mysterious undertone, as if he were seeking to establish a private understanding.

" Delicious soup *bisque* is !"

" *A la reine* is better," replied Colonel Pycherly, who had overheard the whispered remark, and who had already reached the gilt cipher at the bottom of his plate.

" You should have sent word to Mrs. Arden," maliciously responded Mrs. Tinedale, one of whose favourite diversions consisted in bullying Colonel Pycherly.

"Eh—what—I beg pardon," replied Colonel Pycherly, made aware that he had committed some blunder, by her provoking smile. And turning very red, he applied himself diligently to discussing some turbot *á la crême*, which here providentially made its appearance.

Mrs. Tinedale's face assumed an expression of

content. She never undertook a conversation with any pleasant man at dinner, until she had silenced all the stupid ones within reach. She waited quietly a while for an opportunity to demolish young Renson, but he was on his guard and prudently held his tongue. She was obliged to give him up.

"It is a long time since you were in England, before, is it not?" she said to Mr. Hungerford.

"Nearly three years."

"Does not a civilized table look very strangely to you?"

"Somewhat."

"Is it true that one grows so fond of the sort of life you have been leading, that one gives it up unwillingly?"

"I can imagine it might be so."

"But how do you find it yourself?"

"Really, I can scarcely tell."

Edith heaved an inaudible sigh.— "Mr. Hungerford wouldn't talk— it was just as Walter had predicted."—

Mrs. Tinedale understood Mr. Hungerford's reserve to mean that he wanted to eat his dinner, and would not talk until he chose; so she turned to Walter.

" You must allow me to congratulate you on Miss Arden's recovery. How charmingly she is looking to-night."

" Yes. She is well again," he replied.

" Are you quite well again, my dear ? " asked Lady Emily, raising her voice and addressing Edith. " What a dreadful thing it was !"

Mr. Hungerford looked up enquiringly.

" A shocking fright she had. How can Lady Emily refer to it ?" Mrs. Tinedale said, in a low tone.

" Excuse me," he said, suppressing his voice, " but you excite my curiosity."

" It happened at a show. Miss Hartley took her there in one of her freaks. They let out an American panther. It sprang at her."

" An unpardonable thing to let such an animal loose. They are untameable."

" And such a lovely young creature as that,"
responded Mrs. Tinedale, warmly.

Mr. Hungerford looked at her. She was not
jealous of a prettier woman than herself. He
liked her. He would talk; but later. He was
not going to harangue a dinner table.

" Pray where were you at this time last year?"
asked Walter, mindful of Edith's delight in
hearing clever men talk, and making a forlorn
effort to gratify it.

" Last October, at this time, I was in Canada."

" I have heard that there are such lovely
flowers in Canada," said Mrs. Tinedale, promptly
returning to the charge, " quite different from
any we have here. Is it true?"

" I found some specimens that I thought
valuable, in the lands of the Assiniboines and of
the Arramahoos."

" Would you not describe to me some of the
strangest you saw? I will have them made up
for a ball dress. I hate to wear what everyone
else does. I'm sick of roses and forget-me-nots,

and lilies of the valley, and eglantine. I should be so glad to have something new."

" I have some drawings at Mr. Tracey's, which I should be happy to show you," replied Mr. Hungerford, looking super-eminently bored, as he perceived that the whole table was listening to him, " but really I'm sorry to say that I can't undertake to describe a flower so that it could be made available for the purpose you mention." Herewith he helped himself largely to some *crême á la Venise*, a wonderful compound, raised upon a basis of pounded chicken.

" What a bear ! " thought Mrs. Tinedale, and she betook herself to listening to her neighbours.

" I've not seen you at any of the meets," said young Renson, who now prepared himself for an attack in form, addressing Edith. " I'm sure you ride."

"A little."

" Oh, but it must be more than a little, if you're going to be here long. And Arden, he hasn't been out this season."

"I do not know how long I shall be here," said Edith.

—How painful the thought of going away had become. She wished she could always stay at the Hall.—She looked up and catching Walter's eye, looked hastily away again.

"Arden rides famously; you must get him to give you lessons, to bring you into training, you know. Our meets are capital. It's a bore to miss them."

"I don't think I should enjoy them," replied Edith.

" Oh, but you couldn't help it, you know. It's the one thing worth having : —a scamper across country for hours, half the hunt thrown out, only a few stragglers in at the death ; it's quite glorious, you know."

" Is it? " answered Edith, incredulously.

" Only a lady must have a horse that understands his business, that won't baulk at a ditch, nor hang his hind legs on a gate. Arden's horses are good, but I should think rather hard on the bit for a lady.    I've a lovely little mare, just the thing for you.    I should be so glad if you'd let me send her over."

" You needn't be in hopes that Miss Arden is in need of Patsy," said Mrs. Tinedale.    " She rides Moira, and she has Mrs. Lacy's pony, too. Mrs. Arden bought it two months ago."

" Oh, but really, do you ride Moira?    Then I quite wonder at your saying you ride a little."

" She is very gentle."

" Perhaps you think so, but I should have said she was a perfect devil."

" Don't talk that way, Renson, you'll frighten Miss Arden," said Walter, glancing at Edith.

"All I can say is, once I said to Miss Hartley that her horse seemed as tame as a cow, and she asked me to change for five minutes, and at the end of three I was in a ditch, and I'm not particularly awkward on horseback either."

" No, that you're not," said young Arden, good naturedly.    " But how did it happen?"

"I don't know.    And there she stood looking

at me and shook her head, and kept just out of reach, and led me that way a mile and a half."

"Who? Miss Hartley?" asked Lady Emily.

"No, the mare. And Miss Hartley quizzed me about it every time she saw me, till something else put it out of her head."

"Yes, I am sure she gave you full measure," said Mrs. Tinedale, laughing. "You should have been photographed as you lay in the ditch, with Moira looking at you. What a run that photograph would have had! I would have given two guineas for one."

And she laughed again.

"She's never easy except when she's plaguing some one," said Mr. Renson, in a sulky undertone to Edith, pouring down a glass of champagne.

"Pray do you ride every day?" he asked, after a short interval.

"Yes, except when it rains."

"Then I shall be on the look out, At what time do you usually go?"

"After lunch," answered Edith, secretly determining to take all her future rides before that hour.

"Ah, then I shall have a good chance of meeting you. It's scarc ely fair, when there are so few ladies, that Arden should have you all to himself."

And so the dinner dragged its slow length along, to the accompaniment of Mr. Renson's pointless sallies and clumsy compliments, for with the champagne that young gentleman's courage rose.

When the ladies returned to the drawing-room, Lady Tremyss sat down behind the stand upon which was placed Isabel's basket, filled with flowers. She bent over it a moment, then signed to Edith to come to her.

"Would you be so kind as to order this basket to be taken away? There is something here that gives me the headache."

Edith rang and gave the desired order, then ensconced herself in a recess, to rally from Mr. Renson's conversation, whilst the ladies talked *chiffons,* as women generally do when men are not present, and occasionally when they are. When the gentlemen returned from the dining-room, Mr. Hungerford came towards her. Lady Tremyss, who was at a little distance, rose and moved away to a shaded part of the room.

Mr. Hungerford's eye followed and dwelt upon Lady Tremyss observantly. Edith perceived it.

" I never saw Lady Tremyss look as she does to-night," she said, glancing at her, as she sat in the shade, the diamonds on her neck and arms sending forth their bright, unquiet reflections. " Her features look more stern, more sharply cut than I have ever seen them."

" A beautiful woman; but not a beauty that I admire," said Mr. Hungerford. " I should almost think—"

He stopped.

"Think what?" asked Edith.

" It is too wild a fancy to put into words," he replied. Then turning to Mr. Tracey, who ap-proached at that moment, he said,

" Do you know that you are in for a breakfast to Mrs. Tinedale ?   I have promised to show her my drawings."

" She shall be welcome to bachelor's fare," responded Mr. Tracey, whose rubicund face and rotund figure bore witness to none of the implied inferiority of the culinary department of a bachelor's establishment.  " And will Miss Arden be bribed by the drawings into doing me the same honour ?"

Pressed by Mr. Hungerford, Edith accepted.

" Two ladies already.   I feel quite flattered.   I think we must make an affair of it, Hungerford. I don't often get such a chance."

And Mr. Tracey laughed as though he found something extremely hilarious in the idea ; then rolling away, he proceeded to dispense his invitations in all quarters for breakfast the next day but one.

Mr. Renson came up as Mr. Tracey retired.

" Immensely nice flowers these are," he observed, surveying the vases on a table near Edith.

" I suppose you are fond of flowers; all young ladies are."

" I like everything in its place," replied Edith coldly, a reply whereat Mr. Hungerford smiled, and Mr. Renson felt uncomfortable, he did not exactly know why.    He glanced around the room.

" How glum Arden looks to-night," he re- marked, with that intuitive and quite astonishing penetration which young men usually display with regard to each other.  " I wonder if anything has gone wrong."

"Have you been talking to him ?" asked Edith, half looking at him with drooping eyelashes. " If so, you know more about it than I do."

" No ; but I think I will," replied young Ren- son, vaguely feeling himself in danger, and beat- ing a precipitate retreat.

Mr. Hungerford laughed when Mr. Renson was out of hearing.

" Are you often so severe ?" he asked, " really you don't look it."

" I don't like young men," answered Edith, with one of the quiet, half sarcastic smiles she could give on occasion.

" I hope you except your brother. He is one of the finest young fellows I ever saw."

Edith flushed a little.

" He is only my cousin, or rather my aunt's nephew," she replied.

" I condole with you, then, on not having such a brother."

Edith glanced at Walter. He was talking with young Renson, and somebody else whose name she had forgotten.—He did look very grave certainly. What could be the matter with him ?—

" He is just as kind as if he were my brother," she answered, " so I don't lose anything."

And she flushed again at the thought of all her causes of gratitude to him.

As Edith turned her head, she saw Lady Tremyss' eye fixed sidelong upon her and her companion. There was something disagreeably keen and piercing in the glance : she moved for-

ward so as to escape it, though by so doing she
abandoned Mr. Hungerford. She passed Walter
on her way towards her aunt. She hoped that
he would speak a word ; but no ;—he did not
even raise his eyes. She sat down near Mrs.
Arden, and remained under her wing until Walter
came up.

" Mr. Hungerford is talking in a way that you
would like to hear. Mrs. Tinedale has got hold
of him, and has drawn him out."

He led Edith to a chair near Mrs. Tinedale's
sofa. Mr. Hungerford was talking to her. People
were standing around, listening.

—" I had seen from the other bank some high
land rising above the trees. My guides told me
that the stronghold of the Arramahoos was built
on it, so I made as straight for it as I could."

" I should have thought you would have been
frightened to death," exclaimed Mrs. Tinedale.

Mr. Hungerford smiled.

" I can't say that I felt quite at my ease. At
length I climbed up the rocks and got into a

deserted fort lined with wigwams. I found one old Indian ill with fever ; not another soul was to be seen. There was food in the different wigwams, so I made myself at home. As to the old man, I undertook to cure him. It wasn't particularly easy as I had to force the quinine down his throat, but he was grateful enough when he began to mend. After four or five days, the rest of the tribe returned. They took my presence in dudgeon, and would have made an end of me had it not been for my old man. He took me under his protection, and finally smuggled me off."

"How did he manage it?" asked Mrs. Tinedale.

"He did it very cleverly. He hid me in the wigwam sacred to the spirits of the dead. No Indian dared come near it, so I was quite safe there. It was a curious place, by the way, all hung round with long locks of hair. One thing that I found rather unpleasant was the seeing a tress of long, reddish golden hair, and be-

side it some shorter black curls, both European,
I am convinced."

" How could they have come there?" asked Mrs.
Tindale.

" My old man told me that they belonged to a
white man and woman who had come to the tribe
many moons ago, and had died not long after
their arrival.    After their death, locks of their
hair had been  hung up as the  customary peace
offering to Manitou."

" And is that all you know ?" inquired Edith.

" Every syllable.   The old man succeeded in
smuggling me across the river, and that is the
last I have seen  of the  Arramahoos," said Mr.
Hungerford, who  seemed of opinion  that he had
absorbed   the   attention  of the  company  long
enough.   He  got  up  and  went  to talk to
Mrs. Arden ; Edith was consequently obliged
to resign herself to be talked to by people she did
not care about, for the  rest of the  evening; en-
during, *tant bien que mal*, the tedium of a country
dinner party.

As the last carriage rolled away, Walter came back into the drawing-room.

" It went off very well, I think ; very well," said Mrs. Arden, in the satisfied tone of a hostess who has done her duty, and feels that nothing more will be expected of her for six weeks to come.

" Yes, it was very nice," answered Edith, fortunately oblivious, for the moment, of all save the traveller. " Mr. Hungerford is delightful ; but, Walter, I am afraid you have not been enjoying yourself."

" Why, what's the matter ?" said Mrs. Arden, suddenly turning upon her nephew.

" I know," said Edith.

" What is it then, my dear ?"

" He has a headache. He is pale ; don't you see it ?"

" And that champagne won't make it any better," responded Mrs. Arden reproachfully. " How could you taste it, Walter, with a headache ?"

Walter, after a rapid survey of circumstances,

thought it better to let it pass as a headache. And this he did; nor, engrossed as his mind was by its new emotions, did that evening's conversation again return to his memory, until recalled by circumstances which he was at that time very far from anticipating.

## CHAPTER IX.

Isabel made her appearance on the following morning somewhat later than usual.

" What do you think?" was her greeting to Edith. " I want to do something, and Mamma won't let me! She actually said no!" Isabel's face expressed the profoundest astonishment.

" Is it the first time she ever said so?" asked Edith.

" The very first time in my life. I can't understand it at all."

She sat down, looking greatly disconcerted.

" What was it about?"

" This morning a note came from Mr. Tracey to me asking me to go to his breakfast with Mamma, and saying that I should see Mr. Hungerford's drawings. I wanted to go because he's a dear old soul and I love him ; and, besides, I wish to see the drawings. I told Mamma so, and she said that she had changed her mind, (for she had accepted, you know), and wasn't going. Then I said I should like to go with Mrs. Arden and you—and she said ' No! ' "

" Did she give you no reason? Didn't she talk with you about it ?"

" Mamma? She never talks to me. I talk to her, and she answers."

" With whom does she talk, then ?" asked Edith, surprised. She had supposed that Isabel and her mother were on the same terms as other mothers and daughters.

" She never talks to anybody. She doesn't like to talk."

" How does she spend her time ?" pursued Edith, who was in an investigating mood.

" She embroiders almost all the time; sometimes she reads. When there's any new book of travels sent down, she reads that."

" And she rides?"

" Oh, yes. She hates driving, but we ride together every day about sunset, you know."

" I must not forget to tell you," interrupted Edith. " I am going to take all my rides after breakfast in future."

" Then I shall come in the afternoon. But why do you change?"

" Mr. Renson wants to ride with us."

" Does he want to get on Moira again?" inquired Isabel, her eyes sparkling mischievously.

" I fancy not. He told us of his mishap, and how you laughed at him."

" He was made to be laughed at. Why, do you know, he used to be such a figure before he had Storrord! Once I counted the stripes on his trousers. It didn't take long, there were only two and a half all the way down. And he wore red neckcloths and yellow waistcoats."

" He was dressed like any one else last night."

" Oh, but I told you Storrord keeps him in capital order."

"Who is Storrord?"

"His valet. He used to be Sir Ralph's. I was glad to have him go. He always looked like a Jesuit in disguise. Melvil used to say that he heard through the doors and walls. He knew everything. All the servants were afraid of him, except Goliath."

"I am so sorry you can't go to-morrow," said Edith, who did not care to think of Goliath.

"Yes. But there is one good side to it. Mamma told me to invite you to come and dine at the Park the next day, I suppose to console me, for I was immensely disappointed. You must come. I've been here almost every day since you were ill, and you've only been once to see me."

Accustomed as Edith was to the modern elegance of Arden Court, and the old-fashioned comfort of the Hall, the formal magnificence of the Park rather oppressed her. Its length of dark corridors, its endless ranges of rooms,—some of them never used, but, like all the rest, kept in scrupulous order,—filled with antique plenishing, and shown in detail by Isabel, who seemed determined to make her friend as well acquainted with the premises as she was herself, rather depressed Edith; they suggested all sorts of gloomy fancies, the more depressing, perhaps, because so utterly unshared by her companion. At last she expressed an unwillingness to explore any further, and proposed a return to Isabel's own room.

"One moment," said Isabel, unclosing a door. "I want you to see Lady Anne's chamber."

She drew Edith within a room larger and more richly furnished than any they had seen.

"This is very handsome," said Edith, looking at the satin bed in its tarnished gilt alcove, the toilette glass of chiselled silver, the ebony wardrobe whereon was carved St. Michael struggling with the fiend, and the stained glass in the oriel window which projected boldly over the terrace. "I should think it would still be used."

L 5

"It hasn't been used for two hundred and fifty years," replied Isabel, impressively, "not since Lady Anne died in that bed."

"But why?" asked Edith, glancing at the alcove. It was not precisely agreeable to be brought in fancy so near the long vanished occupant.

"Why? Because she murdered her husband in this very room. Sit down and I'll tell you about it."

She drew Edith to a great yellow easy chair, and sat down on the floor before her.

"Lady Anne was a great heiress, you must know, and a very haughty sort of woman. She had refused numbers of lovers, but at length she married Sir Hilary, who wasn't a particularly good sort of man. She was dreadfully jealous of him, but it was ever so long before she found out anything. However, one evening she was sitting in that window, and she looked out and saw Sir Hilary walking cautiously down the terrace. He turned the corner of the house, after looking all around as if to be sure that nobody saw him. Lady Anne hurried along the gallery, and looked out of a loop hole in the tower at the end, and there he **was** talking with one of her women, and she saw him kiss her. Then she went back and sat down again as if nothing had happened. **And** that **night** she poisoned Sir Hilary, and everybody thought he had died in a fit; but what she did to the maid was worse. She took her into a lonely room, and tied her hand and foot, and locked her up in a closet, and starved her to death. Then she took away the key of the room, and nobody ever found it out till after Lady Anne was dead."

" How did they find it out, then?" asked Edith.

" If you will believe it, she had left a written confession of the whole in that wardrobe, where they found it after she was dead."

" I can imagine that the solitude of her crime was too much to bear," replied Edith, thoughtfully ; then rising quickly, " I don't want to think how she felt," she said. "It seems to make me feel wicked too."

"You wicked!" said Isabel, rising to her knees, and gazing steadfastly into Edith's face. "You couldn't feel wicked if you tried—I wish I couldn't."

She turned away, and walked with Edith silently down the gallery to her own room.

"What do you mean by saying you might feel wicked?" said Edith, seating herself caressingly by Isabel.

"You couldn't understand," replied Isabel, turning away her face.

"I am fond of you, and that would help me to understand," answered Edith.

"Are you really, really fond of me?" exclaimed Isabel, throwing her arms around Edith.

"Yes."

"And you won't think the worse of me?"

"How unjust that would be."

"Then I'll tell you.—Sometimes I feel as if I should stifle to death, as if I should die. I long to tear this life from me, and to rush forth I don't know where. I dream of great plains and snow fields, and of being borne across them like the wind, and there is fire in me and I feel no cold. I want to be free. I don't want to be good and go to church and live among quiet people. I want,—oh, I don't know what I want,"

And Isabel threw herself down, pressed her face into Edith's lap, and burst into a passion of tears.

The wild words, the stormy self-abandonment, awoke a responsive trouble in Edith's thoughts. Hitherto unfelt chords within her vibrated to Isabel's impetuous, imploring voice.—What could she say to her?—She could think of nothing. Before she knew it her own tears were flowing, she could not tell why.

The unreasoning sympathy seemed to calm Isabel. She rose from her position, and sat quietly down beside Edith. They had not yet spoken when the dinner bell rang.

" Oh, there's dinner. Do I look as if I had

been crying?" exclaimed Isabel, running to the glass; then turning to Edith, she displayed her brilliant colour and hazel eyes, as fresh and bright as if she had never shed a tear.

"Come—I did not hear the first bell, did you? We were in the old rooms, I fancy."

She hurried with Edith down the gallery.

Edith's heart rather failed her as she entered the great dining-room, the same where she and Isabel had chased the mole, and where, lifting the carpet, they had seen that dark, wide-spreading stain. She glanced at the spot. Upon it stood Goliath with his Herculean form and ghastly scar. She was internally thankful that she was placed at table so that he was not within her sight.

Isabel's mood had changed. She chattered without cessation during the whole of the dinner, she told the most absurdly improbable stories, most of them invented expressly for the occasion; she mimicked all her acquaintance in turn, and ended with a charity sermon from the rector,

delivered with such ludicrous accuracy of imitation as to send the statue-like footmen into
inward agonies, and to bring a smile over the
grim visage of Goliath.

Edith was in momentary expectation that
Isabel would receive some reproof from Lady
Tremyss, but no word of counsel or disapproba-
tion crossed her hostess's lips. She sat a quiet
spectator of her daughter's vagaries, without in
any way attempting to check them.

At length Isabel talked herself out, as she expressed it, and applying to Edith, demanded an
exact account of the breakfast at Mr. Tracey's.

" It was very pleasant indeed," answered Edith.

" Yes, but that isn't enough. You must
begin at the beginning. Who were there ?"

" Every one, excepting Lady Tremyss, who
was at the Hall, and quite a number of people
beside."

" There couldn't have been any dancing, of
course," said Isabel. " I love dancing. Mamma,
when I'm seventeen you must give a ball."

" If you wish it," replied Lady Tremyss.

" I never thought of it before, but I do wish
it, and you're a love to say I may have it ; but
we'll talk about that by-and-by ;—now we'll
listen to the breakfast."

" As soon as breakfast was over we went into
the drawing-room, and Mr. Hungerford showed
us his drawings."

" Were they very beautiful ? Mr. Tracey said
they were quite different from anything in England. Is it true ?"

" Yes, quite."

" I wish I had seen them. Did you ever see
any like them before ?"

Edith hesitated. She had seen some flowers
like Mr. Hungerford's before, but an inexplicable
unwillingness made her reluctant to say where.
She had intended to tell Isabel, but now that she
was with her and her mother, she felt her tongue
tied.

" Yes, you have, I see. Where were they ?"

" I thought some of them were like the

flowers on your basket," she answered reluctantly.

"What, the flowers Mamma drew? How strange. Why Mamma, how learned you are! Where did you find them?"

"There are some engravings in the library that you can look at with Miss Arden, after dinner. Perhaps those are like Mr. Hungerford's."

"I never saw them," answered Isabel, "Where are they?"

"On the highest shelf, between the windows."

"Oh, I can't reach there; the steps are not tall enough for me; but I'll have them got down. It is odd they should be there. All the other engravings are below."

As soon as they rose from table, Isabel led Edith into the library.

It was a large room, so dark in its colouring that the light of the fire and of the two wax candles that stood in solemn solitude on the great green table, did but illuminate a small circle of the surrounding space. Their rays, brightly pro-

jected at first, soon died away, leaving in shadow
the great bookcases with their piled-up treasures,
and the bronze busts which looked gravely down
from the top of their heavy cornices. Edith
wondered, as she looked round, whether Sir Ralph
used often to sit there, and what books he used
to read.

Isabel answered the unexpressed question.

" I don't often come here. It is the only place
in the house that makes me think of Sir Ralph.
He was always shut up here, poring over his
books, while Mamma sat at her embroidery in
that window. One day I climbed up and peeped
in at the other window as I went down the
terrace. He wasn't reading, he was staring at
her. She didn't see him. He had on such a
face !"

" What sort of face ?"

" He had bitten his lip till it was white, and
his brows were all scowling ; and as I was peep-
ing I saw him pass his hand across his forehead
two or three times, as if he couldn't bear what

he was thinking about. It was queer, for Mamma looked handsomer than ever that day. She was dressed in white, and I had stuck a red rose in her hair when she went down."

" Then you used to have her with you sometimes ?"

" Oh, yes. She always came into my room, and had her hair done there, and sat with me while I took my breakfast, before she went down. After breakfast she used to sit with him a while, and then she would come upstairs and stay with me ever so long. I know he didn't like it. Storrord told Melvil that he had heard Sir Ralph curse awfully at me when Mamma was with me and he thought nobody heard him, but he never prevented it. I don't believe he would have dared to try. He always seemed afraid of Mamma."

" Afraid of his own wife !"

" He never could bear to have her look at him, so the servants said. I don't know much about it. I was never with them. But I know that he never, even at table, sat opposite to her, though he used to keep her beside him as much as he could."

" How very peculiar," Edith remarked.

" Yes, it was one of his whims. He was full of them. He hated the dark. The house used always to be lighted before sunset. Anybody would have said he thought there were ghosts in it. But I'm forgetting what we came for. Now let us see the engravings."

The portfolio of engravings was brought from the shelf. It was a very old one, and the engravings were spotted and defaced as if by age. They represented birds and flowers grouped together.

" Many of these are like Mr. Hungerford's," said Edith; " and see, here is the scarlet flower on your basket, and there, look—is not that the white, crown-shaped one?"

" Oh, yes, and I know this one, and this, and this, " exclaimed Isabel, rapidly turning them over; " and these birds. Why, Mamma is embroidering some of them now. There's her blue bird, and her crimson-breasted bird, and her hawk. Come and see."

She hurried Edith into the drawing-room, where, by a stand with candles, Lady Tremyss sat bending over a frame.

"Oh, Mamma, we've found your birds; I want Edith to see them. Look."

Turning back the frame, she displayed a group of singular force of design and colouring. A blue jay had swooped upon an oriole, which, mortally wounded, its feathers torn, was dying in its assailant's grasp; while above, a black hawk, with closed wings and inverted head, was dropping unseen upon the victorious marauder.

"How life-like that is. I can hear the poor bird's last gasp," said Edith, compassionately. "How treacherous and cruel the blue bird looks. I am glad the black hawk is near," she added, with a sudden change of tone.

A long ray of light shot from Lady Tremyss' eye; then she silently returned the frame to its place, and bent over it again.

"Now let us finish looking over the engravings," said Isabel.

They went back to the library.

As they turned over the last sheet, Isabel pushed aside the portfolio.

"Now that we have seen those and found out where Mamma gets her designs, let us talk about the ball. This house will be nice for it, won't it? We can have how many rooms open? There's the hall—but that won't count—the drawing-room, the dining-room, the library, and the dancing-room—that's four. That's enough, I think."

Edith agreed that it would be enough.

"I don't mean to have flowers everywhere," continued Isabel. "I won't have the house look as if it were all conservatory. That would not be in *its* style at all. I will have the rooms just as they are, only as light as day; all but the dancing-room. I mean to have that filled with flowers. But you haven't seen it. I'll show it to you."

Isabel tried to open a door. It was
locked. She rang for the key. The door was
unclosed. A long black vista lay beyond. She
took one of the candlesticks from the table, and,
calling to Edith to follow her, advanced into the
room.

It had the chilly and ghostlike look of all uninhabited apartments. It was of great length,
but not of corresponding height. At intervals
along the walls were placed mirrors ; the floor
was of polished oak.

"Wont it be nice for dancing?" exclaimed
Isabel. "See, there are the guests already coming
to meet us."

She smiled and nodded to the multiplied
reflections of her figure in the mirrors around.
The reflections, coming out of the darkness beyond,
smiled and nodded back with a strange, unreal
mirth.

Isabel set the candlestick upon the ground.

"Come, let us waltz once round to see how
nice it will be when it is all full of flowers and
music and people."

And catching Edith around the waist, she whirled her about the room till they were forced to stop from want of breath.

As Isabel released her, Edith staggered back and leaned against the wall.

"Oh!" exclaimed Isabel, penitently, "I hope I haven't tired you out."

"I am only a little giddy. It will pass in a moment," replied Edith. "But what is that sound?" she said, after a moment's pause, standing up erect.

Isabel laid her head where Edith's had rested. There was a sound as of distant hammering.

"Why, where can it be? It can't come from upstairs—the picture gallery is over this room, Nor from the cellars, for they are under another part of the house."

"If it were from upstairs, it would sound nearer," said Edith. "It seems a great way off."

"I'll call Mamma," said Isabel. "Perhaps it's the ghost of Lady Anne's maid."

She ran away to summon her mother.

Lady Tremyss came gliding in her sweeping

black dress, up the length of the room. She stood where Edith had stood, and listened.

"Send Goliath," she said; "but Isabel, Miss Arden and you must not stay here any longer; you will both take cold."

The girls returned to the library.

As Goliath approached his mistress, she pointed to the wall.

"Stand there. Do you hear that? It must be stopped."

"I have tried. It cannot be helped, my lady."

Lady Tremyss, followed by Goliath, left the dancing-room without another word.

"What is it, Mamma?" asked Isabel, as her mother passed through the library.

"Rats," Lady Tremyss answered.

## CHAPTER X.

In such natures as Edith Arden's, it is suffering only that awakens passion. As yet she dwelt in the tranquil world of sentiment. Not from any lack of native force. The vivid eye, the thin nostril, the deeply cut lips, all revealed a latent strength capable of being stimulated into vehemence; but that strength lay sleeping in the quiet recesses within.

So the autumn days passed on, each hour bringing her unconsciously closer to Walter, her unfailing companion in her rides and walks and drives. She forgot her dreary childhood, its loneliness, its grief; she did not remember the separation from the Hall, which must inevitably come at last; no cloud cast its shadow over that golden spring time of her life. Edith was happy.

One result of the morning rides referred to was, to bring Isabel to the Hall in the afternoon, and consequently to throw her much into Walter's society.

In young Arden's newly awakened tenderness, his tone had become gentler to all; and it scarcely needed Edith's warmly expressed conviction that Isabel possessed much more feeling and mind than she was in the habit of showing, to sensibly modify his tone towards her. His respect for what Edith esteemed, was heightened into something very like friendship, by his sympathy with Isabel's adoring affection.

So Isabel came over each afternoon, and sat with Edith, and listened while Walter read aloud or talked, and grew quieter and gentler every day. Her intellect seemed to have received some sudden impetus. It developed rapidly. Her very appearance began to change. Her eyes grew deeper, her smile became less frequent, and more thoughtful. Her former glitter and glow was settling into a steadier lustre, more grateful to eye and sense.

Some weeks had thus passed, when Edith became aware of Isabel's possession of a talent whose existence she had not suspected. She had several times, in the earlier days of their acquaintance, asked her for music. Isabel had always refused, excusing herself on various pleas, till Edith had almost forgotten that she had the power.

One afternoon Isabel had been unusually serious. Walter was away; she was alone with Edith. After sitting a while silent, she opened the pianoforte and began to play. Edith laid down her book, and listened with a mixture of surprise and delight, which gradually changed into distress. Isabel was playing Russian airs, full of sighing disquiet, of restless pain.

The sun had sunk behind a cloud, a melancholy wind was sighing through the trees; its mournful symphony filled up the pauses of Isabel's wordless plaint.

" Oh, hush ; I can't bear it ; I can't bear it ! " Edith at last passionately exclaimed.

Isabel paused, and leaning her head upon the pianoforte, sat without speaking ; for the first time heedless of her friend. Then she left the instrument and glided away, pressing a kiss upon Edith's forehead as she passed the sofa where she lay, her face buried in her hands.

No sooner was Isabel gone than Edith rose, hurried into her own room, locked the door, and sat down to think. Her cheeks were burning, her heart was trobbing.—What had she felt! what had she thought! She had longed to turn from the yearning entreaty of the music, to turn and throw herself on Walter's breast!—

The wind had risen and brought with it clouds, heavy and storm laden. For three days the rain fell without intermission, lashing the panes, and sweeping wildly away over the lawn.

Walter had hoped for still more unbroken companionship with Edith, now that they were fellow prisoners in the Hall, but to his surprise and displeasure she evinced a sudden preference for his aunt's society. She clung persistently to Mrs. Arden's side, and tacitly refused all continuance of that solitary converse with him which had recently formed so great a pleasure in his life.

Mrs. Arden came to the conclusion that Edith was getting a little tired of being so much with Walter, and did her best to amuse her, secretly wishing that the weather would clear up and bring Isabel. She liked Isabel much better now that she was quieter, and could sit still and talk like a reasonable being.

On the fourth day the rain ceased, the wind fell, the sun shone out, and brought Isabel, delighted at her release from the Park.

"My dear," said Mrs. Arden to Edith, "I think you had better put on your habit and take a little ride with Isabel, I do indeed. You're not looking quite so well as you did, and as I like to see you. I know what you want, but there's no use thinking of that," she added, regretfully, "and so you'd better go out, you really had, to ride. Walter will go too, I dare say. It will do you good to get a little fresh air."

"Yes, do come. It is warm as midsummer," added Isabel.

The horses were ordered, and they left the Hall. They rode through the wooded lanes, already beginning to dry, but in their deep gullies and tiny water-courses showing how violent had been the recent storm. The trunks of the trees were dark with moisture, and ever and anon a few lingering drops fell on the heads of the riders, as a startled bird sprang from some little bough above them. The sun shot long, slanting rays of light over the vivid green of the fields, and sprinkled golden dust upon the crumbling ridges of the ploughed lands.

They rode on for a while almost in silence, enjoying the subdued beauty of the scene and the

warmth of the sunny air.    At length Isabel suddenly exclaimed,

"I knew I had something to tell you.    Just
fancy, Mamma won't have the dancing-room
used!"

"That's a pity," replied Edith; "it is such a
nice room."

"Yes.    I had set my heart on it, and I never
imagined I couldn't have it; but this morning
when I asked Mamma how many camellias we
should want for it, she said it was not to be
thrown open, but that the dancing would be
in the great room opening out of the dining-
room."

"I dare say it will do quite as well," responded
Edith, consolingly.

"Oh, but I assure you you're mistaken!    It
hasn't any mirrors at all, and a dancing-room
needs them.    It is so very strange—Mamma has
contradicted me twice lately, once about the
breakfast, and now about this.    I can't think
what it means."

They had reached the river as she was speaking, and were crossing the bridge.

" Look there !" exclaimed Isabel, interrupting herself. She laughed and pointed with her riding whip. " Just look at their funny little heads."

Edith looked, and saw not far from them a number of children's faces looking up from the river, with staring eyes and laughing mouths. The little bathers had crouched under the water until the party should have past by.

" Little rascals, they oughtn't to be there," said Walter. " The river is very full, and—"

Shrill cries rose as he spoke, from the water two little pink arms were seen struggling wildly a moment, then they disappeared.

Walter leaped from his horse, threw aside his coat and boots, and sprang on the parapet. He stood for an instant, the noble proportions of his figure displayed against the sky. The little head appeared an instant, then sank again. Walter plunged in. As he flung himself down, all the colour left Edith's cheeks and lips. She closed her eyes. Isabel urged her horse close to the parapet, and leaned over, watching the swimmer. The child rose twice again before he could reach him. As he sank the third time, young Arden dived. He re-appeared, bearing a helpless little burden.

It was hard work, swimming with one hand against a river running like a mill-course; but he gained the bank, and gave his insensible charge into the hands of a woman who came running from a cottage on the bank.

After assuring himself that the child had received no harm, Walter returned to his companions. Edith received him in silence; Isabel, with a few hurried words, held out the reins of his horse.

" Much obliged," he said gaily, hastily resuming his discarded articles of attire, and springing into the saddle. " It's lucky that Roy didn't take himself off. What an opportunity he lost !" He laughed, and patted the horse's neck. Isabel thought she had never seen him look half so handsome.

The groom came leisurely into sight at that moment. Setting spurs to his horse, he galloped up.

" Now I shall go home, and you will go back with Edith. She looks ready to faint."

Isabel struck her horse a sharp blow, and dashed away, followed by the groom.

" Were you frightened?" said Walter, bending over Edith's saddle-bow, as they turned their horses' heads homeward.

" I,—yes,—no,—I mean I was afraid the little boy would be drowned," replied Edith, with that instinctive duplicity with which even the most candid of her sex will seek to hide her emotions from him who is the cause of them.

Walter, thus repulsed, rode on beside her without a word, until they reached the Hall.

Mrs. Arden was sitting reading at the drawing-room window. She came out in tremulous haste.

" Oh, Walter! dear, dear me, what is the matter? You're all dripping wet. What is it? Tell me quick. Are you sure you aren't hurt? Where have you been?"

" Picking a little boy out of the river—that's all," he answered, rather gruffly, lifting Edith from her saddle.

" Oh, what a dreadful risk! Was there any danger? I'm sure there was. I'm trembling all over, only thinking of it. And what would have become of me if anything had happened to you! Oh, Walter, Walter! But where's Edith?"

Edith had disappeared.

END OF VOL. I.

T. C. NEWBY, 30, Welbeck Street, Cavendish Square, London.

# WILSON'S
## PATENT DRAWING-ROOM
# BAGATELLE AND BILLIARD TABLES,
### WITH REVERSIBLE TOPS.
#### Circular, Oblong, Oval, and other Shapes, in various Sizes
##### FORMING A HANDSOME TABLE.

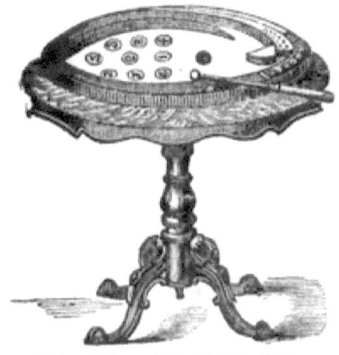 

| Patent Bagatelle Table--Open. | Patent Bagatelle Table--Closed. |

#### Prices from 5 to 25 Guineas.    Prospectus Free by post.

---

## WILSON AND CO., PATENTEES,
#### Cabinet Makers, Upholsterers, House Agents, Undertakers, &c.,
18, WIGMORE STREET (Corner of Welbeck Street), LONDON, W.; also at the
MANUFACTURING COURT, CRYSTAL PALACE, SYDENHAM.

---

### In 1 Vol.   Price 12s.
# ON  CHANGE  OF  CLIMATE,
#### A GUIDE FOR TRAVELLERS IN PURSUIT OF HEALTH.
### By THOMAS MORE MADDEN, M.D., M.R.C.S. Eng.

Illustrative of the Advantages of the various localities resorted to by Invalids, for the cure or alleviation of chronic diseases, especially consumption. With Observations on Climate, and its Influences on Health and Disease, the result of extensive personal experience of many Southern Climes.

#### SPAIN, PORTUGAL, ALGERIA, MOROCCO, FRANCE, ITALY, THE MEDITERRANEAN ISLANDS, EGYPT, &c.

" Dr. Madden has been to most of the places he describes, and his book contains the advantage of a guide, with the personal experience of a traveller. To persons who have determined that they ought to have change of climate, we can recommend Dr. Madden as a guide."—*Athenæum*.

" It contains much valuable information respecting various favorite places of resort, and is evidently the work of a well-informed physician."—*Lancet*.

" Dr. Madden's book deserves confidence—a most accurate and excellent work."—*Dublin Medical Review*.

# TEETH WITHOUT PAIN AND WITHOUT SPRINGS.

## OSTEO EIDON FOR ARTIFICIAL TEETH, EQUAL TO NATURE.

---

Complete Sets £4 4s., £7 7s., £10 10s., £15 15s., and £21.

SINGLE TEETH AND PARTIAL SETS AT PROPORTIONATELY
MODERATE CHARGES.

---

A PERFECT FIT GUARANTEED.

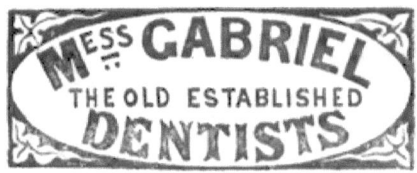

London:

27, HARLEY STREET, CAVENDISH SQUARE, W.
134, DUKE STREET, LIVERPOOL.
65, NEW STREET, BIRMINGHAM.

---

CITY ADDRESS :

64, LUDGATE HILL, 64.

(4 doors from the Railway Bridge).

---

ONLY ONE VISIT REQUIRED FROM COUNTRY PATIENTS.

---

Gabriel's Treatise on the Teeth, explaining their patented mode of supplying Teeth without Springs or Wires, may be had gratis on application, or free by post.

# FAMILY MOURNING.

## MESSRS. JAY

Would respectfully announce that great saving may be made by purchasing Mourning at their Establishment,

### THEIR STOCK OF

# FAMILY MOURNING

### BEING

## THE LARGEST IN EUROPE.

# MOURNING COSTUME

### OF EVERY DESCRIPTION

## KEPT READY-MADE,

And can be forwarded to Town or Country at a moment's notice.

The most reasonable Prices are charged, and the wear of every Article Guaranteed.

## THE LONDON

# GENERAL MOURNING WAREHOUSE,

## 247 & 248, REGENT STREET,

### (NEXT THE CIRCUS.)

## JAY'S.

# BEDSTEADS, BEDDING, AND BED ROOM FURNITURE.

## HEAL & SON'S

Show Rooms contain a large assortment of Brass Bedsteads, suitable both for home use and for Tropical Climates.

Handsome Iron Bedsteads, with Brass Mountings, and elegantly Japanned.

Plain Iron Bedsteads for Servants.

Every description of Woodstead, in Mahogany, Birch, and Walnut Tree Woods, Polished Deal and Japanned, all fitted with Bedding and Furnitures complete.

Also, every description of Bed Room Furniture, consisting of Wardrobes, Chests of Drawers, Washstands, Tables, Chairs, Sofas, Couches, and every article for the complete furnishing of a Bed Room.

AN

## ILLUSTRATED CATALOGUE,

Containing Designs and Prices of 150 articles of Bed Room Furniture, as well as of 100 Bedsteads, and Prices of every description of Bedding

Sent Free by Post.

## HEAL & SON,

### BEDSTEAD, BEDDING,

AND

### BED ROOM FURNITURE MANUFACTURERS

196, TOTTENHAM COURT ROAD

LONDON. W.

THE TOILET.—A due attention to the gifts and graces of the person, and a becoming preservation of the advantages of nature, are of more value and importance with reference to our health and well-being, than many parties are inclined to suppose. Several of the most attractive portions of the human frame are delicate and fragile, in proportion as they are graceful and pleasing ; and the due conservation of them is intimately associated with our health and comfort. The hair, for example, from the delicacy of its growth and texture, and its evident sympathy with the emotions of the mind ; the skin, with its intimate relation to the most vital of our organs, as those of respiration, circulation and digestion, together with the delicacy and susceptibility of its own texture ; and the teeth, also, from their peculiar structure, formed as they are, of bone or dentine, and cased with a fibrous investment of enamel ; these admirable and highly essential portions of our frames, are all to be regarded not merely as objects of external beauty and display, but as having an intimate relation to our health, and the due discharge of the vital functions. The care of them ought never to be entrusted to ignorant or unskilful hands ; and it is highly satisfactory to point out as protectors of these vital portions of our frame the preparations which have emanated from the laboratories of the Messrs. Rowlands, their unrivalled Macassar for the hair, their Kalydor for improving and beautifying the complexion, and their Odonto for the teeth and gums.

---

NEW NOVELS IN THE PRESS.

In Three Vols.

# THE MAITLANDS.

In One Vol.  Price 10s. 6d.

# THE ADVENTURES OF A SERF WIFE

## AMONG THE MINES OF SIBERIA.

# J. W. BENSON,

www.ingramcontent.com/pod-product-compliance
Lightning Source LLC
Chambersburg PA
CBHW020357030726
47496CB00007B/2181